Angela Meyer is a Melbourne-based writer and reviewer. Her fiction has been published in *Seizure*, *Wet Ink*, *The Lifted Brow*. She has written on books for many publications including *The Big Issue*, *The Australian*, and *Crikey* and she has interviewed authors at festivals across Australia and overseas. A chapbook of her flash fiction will be published by Inkerman & Blunt in 2014. literaryminded.com.au

The Great Unknown

stories

edited by
Angela Meyer

SPINELESS WONDERS

www.shortaustralianstories.com.au

Spineless Wonders
BN01164417
PO Box 220 STRAWBERRY HILLS
New South Wales, Australia, 2012
www.shortaustralianstories.com.au

First published by Spineless Wonders 2013
The Great Unknown anthology © Spineless Wonders 2013.
Copyright of individual stories remains with the authors

Cover images © Michael Vale 2013

Edited by Angela Meyer. Book design by Bethany Ng.
Copyedited by Bethany Ng and Bronwyn Mehan.

Typeset in Georgia.

Printed and bound by Lightning Source Australia

ISBN 9780987447937 (pbk.)

National Library of Australia Cataloguing-in-Publication
entry:
The Great Unknown/Edited by Angela Meyer
1st ed.
A823.4

This project has been assisted by the Australian Government
through the Australia Council, its arts funding and advisory body.

For Henry Bemis, and everyone who appreciates a quiet moment alone with a book.

Contents

I've long had an interest in the strange, the absurd, the macabre, the speculative and the fantastical. These genres often speak forcefully of reality *because* they depart from it. Think of Orwell's *Nineteen Eighty-Four* or Franz Kafka's personal yet strangely prescient works. Just as often stories in these genres have the purpose of entertainment and escapism — but still act (if done well) to enable the imagination to stretch and entertain ideas of living differently, living curiously, or facing or analysing one's fears.

The stories in this book explore our fascination with the unknown, the mysterious, or even just the slightly *off*. Life itself is strange, and these stories encapsulate the feeling (that we may experience often in Australia, and the world, today) that something is just *not quite right*. And so, besides the unknown, these stories also represent *known*, but often inexpressible, absurdities of everyday life.

They are inspired by shows like *The Twilight Zone*, and its memorable, eerie plotlines — which often contained messages of tolerance, equality, freedom and the dangers of stifling the imagination — beamed into lounge rooms 'down under'. Successors of the show are many, and it is some of these (such as *The X-Files*), or stories of the speculative and uncanny from authors such as Ray Bradbury or Stephen King, that the authors here invoke.

I have no doubt my own interest in these genres partly developed upon my first introduction to *The Twilight Zone*, which was, at ten years old, on the *Tower of Terror* ride at MGM Studios, Disney World, Florida. That was probably when I first heard Rod

Serling's voice inviting me into the Fifth Dimension as I rode in a haunted elevator through the top floor of the Hollywood Tower Hotel, encountering strange visions: doors, figures calling, ticking clocks — that famous music playing — before plunging down thirteen storeys. I took Rod up on his invitation and some of my own first stories were about UFOs, creatures in the woods and magic hats. Of course they were really about family, love and the things I feared most.

A small introduction to the stories themselves: in Paddy O'Reilly's 'Reality TV', a guest is confronted with her husband's infidelity under bright lights, while Ali Alizadeh's 'Truth and Reconciliation' satirises American talk shows and a cultural obsession with sporting 'heroes'. These screen stories play on the idea of what or whose 'reality' is reflected on television. Chris Flynn's 'Sealer's Cove' is joyous fun, about a man on a luxurious nude night-time stroll who encounters some pirates. Krissy Kneen's 'Sleepwalk' leaves a truly spooky after-image on your retina. I dare you to read it before bed, along with Rhys Tate's 'The Koala Motel', where a bloke recounts his story of seeing and hearing *something* at an abandoned motel. The ending will send shivers down your spine.

Carmel Bird evokes Edgar Allan Poe when culture meets nature (and giant hares) in the bush, and a Kubin work is darkly erotic and all-consuming to a young man in Damon Young's *Art*. A Beckettian bird laments its existence in Mark O'Flynn's sharp and absurd 'Bluey and Myrtle', and in the clever and entertaining 'Sticks and Stones', Ryan O'Neill has an academic attacked by a demonic alphabet. A contemporary Burgess Meredith might play the part. Kathy Charles gets the voice of a hard-done-by bloke just right in 'Baby's First Words', where a prescient toddler comes into her own, and a new reality emerges and is shared in Deborah Biancotti's

'See-Saw'. Guy Salvidge's 'A Void' is set in a noiresque retrofuture Melbourne, and in 'The Rift' by Chris Somerville a soldier comes home and is attuned to what the animals know.

A missing family member shows up for dinner in Marion Halligan's evocative story 'Her Dress Was a Pale Glimmer', and in Susan Yardley's 'Significance' a woman literally fades from view. In 'Navigating', by Helen Richardson, a woman is led off track to a spooky but touching dead end. More than one husband has gone missing from The Mistake State Forest, in P. M. Newton's 'The Local', at least that's what you hear at the pub, and vignettes from perpetrator and victim form pieces of a poignant puzzle in A. S. Patrić's 'Memories of Jane Doe'.

The majority of the stories are works by authors invited to contribute to the collection. I was not shy in asking some of my favourite writers — including those who helped to grow my love of short fiction, notably Ryan O'Neill and Paddy O'Reilly — to contribute. They are writers from a range of backgrounds and influences, some of them known for writing 'genre' and others more 'literary', if we want to be basic. There is even a philosopher.

What mattered to me was the quality of their writing, their power of imagination, and an element of darkness, strangeness or the absurd, even in their 'realist' works.

Six of the stories come from the shortlist for the *Carmel Bird Short Fiction Award 2013*, which I had the privilege of judging. The competition authors were given the same brief as the invited, and I was delighted and spooked many times over reading the entries. 'A Cure' by Alexander Cothren stood out for me due to its imaginative speculation on the limits of 'misery' entertainment (and potential abuses of brain-tech), and questions it raises around the effects of saturation and overstimulation. It's an entertaining, smart and emotive story.

I'm grateful to Bronwyn Mehan and Spineless Wonders for trusting me with this project, and I hope you will find it as entertaining and stimulating as I did putting it together. I'm now inviting you, reader, to enter this upside-down land of imagination, in these strange and certainly often frightening times ...

Welcome to *The Great Unknown*,

Angela Meyer

Sleepwalk

Krissy Kneen

Brendan stretched his hand out, expecting to find the warm curve of her back. Her pillow was cold, the blankets kicked back. He blinked into the darkness to see the cold indentation where her body had been. He licked his lips. Brendan was thirsty. They had had a couple of drinks before bed. This, she said, might settle her. Perhaps if she had a few neat measures of Scotch before bed the sleepwalking would stop.

He dragged himself up to sitting, rubbed at his eyes. The curtains were open and there was a vague spill of light, the moon pushing half-heartedly through a scatter of clouds. Brendan could see a faint blue glow from their neighbour's television. The bedside clock clicked over to two a.m. as he watched. He dropped his feet onto the carpet and rubbed them to get the circulation going. There were no lights on in the house. That was the strange thing about her sleepwalking. She seemed to be able to navigate the rooms in the dark.

Brendan flicked a switch and winced, closing his eyes tightly against the rude glare. When he opened them again he could see Emily, a dark shape squatting in the corner of the corridor. He switched on the light and she didn't even flinch. He made his way down the hallway, steadying his sleep-slowed body against the wall with the palm of his hand. She had been sleepwalking for a week now. He first noticed it on Monday when she climbed back into bed, her chilled legs grazing his own, dragging him out of a deep warm dream. Her eyes had been open, her gaze focused a little beyond him, as if, in the world of her night-wandering he was lying a foot or two further away than he was in the waking world. He spoke to her but she didn't seem to hear. She was asleep within seconds, of course she hadn't really ever been awake. Since then, Emily had taken to wandering every night. Sometimes Brendan woke when she came back to bed, sometimes he opened his eyes to see her leaving, her eyes unfocused, her movements slow and precise. He was determined to follow her one night but had not been able to raise the energy to climb out from under the warm blankets in the middle of the morning. You shouldn't wake the sleepwalker when she is on the move. He had read this on the internet. Lots of people sleepwalk. Best thing is to let them have their wander, let them find their own way back to bed.

He stepped quietly up to where she was crouched. Emily's nightdress was long and white with pale embroidery on the hems. Bending like this she looked like a restless spirit. Brendan was careful not to startle her as he tiptoed closer. She had her camera up to her face. This was a surprise. It wasn't her digital camera, but the one her father had given her before he died. His old Lexica through-the-lens. She rarely used it. Most of the jobs she did required her to check the shots immediately. They still had the darkroom set up in the basement but Emily hadn't been in there for years. He was surprised there was even film in the camera. Perhaps there wasn't.

He watched as she adjusted the focus, leaned back, forward, wound the film on and snapped. She stood up. Brendan scrambled to get out of her way. She was agile, even in sleep. She turned on her heel and hurried towards the door to the lounge room.

Brendan flicked the light on. She was taking another photograph. It was a slower process than working with her digital camera, she had to stop to wind the film on. He watched as she took one photo after another, moving around the room as if a model were parading, lying first on the couch, posing by the bookcase then sitting in the upholstered bay window. She was taking the photo shoot very seriously, frowning as she adjusted the framing, measuring the distance between herself and the invisible model by stretching out her arm and then stepping back a pace or two. Brendan had watched her at work once or twice. The same seriousness, the same attention to detail. Terrible to be working all day and to have to turn around and mimic your work at night. It would be awful if he were sleepwalking back to the computer, needlessly working on spreadsheets for hours in the night.

She turned then and looked directly at him. Brendan smiled. Perhaps she had seen him, waking from this strange night-wander. He took a step. It was unsettling that her eyes refused to follow him when he walked towards her. She stared at a fixed point somewhere behind him and when Emily raised her camera, Brendan stepped quickly aside to get out of the shot.

He stood beside her, uncertain as to whether he should touch her, take her by the arm and lead her back to bed. He wanted to cause her the minimum of harm. He stood for a while doing nothing, till – sometime before morning – she placed the camera back on the desk in her study and wandered, blindly and of her own accord, back to bed.

*

Emily shook her head, reading the list of instructions one more time.
 'Aren't people supposed to remember these kinds of things instinctively?' She flattened the page, smoothing it under the palm of her hand.
 'Didn't you do something with the camera in a bag?'
 'That's removing the film. I've already done that. There are two rolls, did you know that? I must have taken a whole roll and got it out of the camera without waking up. The film is probably ruined.'
 She closed the folder, her forehead wrinkled into that old-woman's worry that he found so adorable. He watched as she set up the room, helped her string a piece of twine up in her drying closet, filled a tray with water when she asked him to. The red light from the safe-lamp set off her dark hair. She looked like an actor from a movie and Brendan loved her more, if that was possible. He suspected it wasn't.
 'Nothing.'
 She held the strips of cellulose up to the red lamp and shook her head. 'Blank. Maybe the film was too old. When did I buy it? God. Of course it would be fucked by now.'
 'Or maybe it was dark. I didn't turn the light on till you had been up for a while.'
 'What did I look like? Walking?'
 'Normal.'
 She lifted her hands in a parody of sleepwalk.
 'No. Not like that. Just with a blank expression, or more like unfocused.'
 He opened another bottle of beer and handed it to her. She waved it away with her gloved hand. He felt a drip of chemicals on his arm and wiped it quickly away hoping it wasn't toxic. The room was infused with a sour reek. Brendan knew it probably should be better ventilated. He thought about cancer. His mother had died of it. It was in his genes. He moved away from the trays of chemicals and sat in a corner of the room.

　　　　　　KRISSY KNEEN

'Let there be light!' she said, holding a strip of film up. 'Here.'
She pointed. Brendan moved reluctantly into the halo of fumes.
He remembered his mother arching up on her death bed, her
thin skin tearing and the poisoned blood leaking out. He held
his breath as he leaned in to look at the strip of film. Little
patches of light in darkness, the edge of a lamp? A couch? It was
hard to tell.

'Shouldn't you wear a mask when you do this stuff?' he asked
and she ignored him.

'Don't suppose I'll win any awards with these.'

'Sure you don't want another beer?'

'After.'

And she removed a sheet of card from out of its thick black
plastic sleeve, set it on the enlarger, timing the spill of light. It
was like riding a bike after all; she tipped the trays of chemicals
back and forth, agitating the print, lifting it with tongs and
dropping it into a second tray and a third. She clipped one print
after another to the drying rack. Emily had hit her stride. He
stood behind her and slipped his fingers under the edge of her
shirt. He liked to watch her work. He kissed the nape of her
neck, lifting the spill of her hair and breathing in that sweet mix
of perfume and soil and skin.

'Brendan?'

He let her hair back down and leaned his head on her shoulder.
This is how he saw it first, resting against her skin, feeling the
sudden tensing of the muscles in her neck, the sharp stillness.

She was looking at a photo through a magnifying glass. The
images were hanging at an angle, the edges already beginning to
curl as the surfaces dried unevenly. He saw their life, or pieces of
it in each of the prints, the lamp, the edge of their couch and here,
a blur of grey behind it. The same blur, movement? Something too
fast for the speed of the shutter? This same pale smear repeated
in each of the hanging squares. And then the final image. He
peered into it through her magnifying glass, a corner of a room,
no furniture, only the edge of a painting to indicate where the
photograph had been taken. The dining room near the portrait
of Emily as a child. The figure was a blur, but clearer here,
shoulders, arms, the crouch of legs. The head seemed elongated
as if captured while being shaken from side to side. Only the eyes
were still, enlarged in the circle of the glass. Round, clear, as if for

a fraction of a second the figure had stopped shifting from side to side to stare, unblinking at the camera, at Emily, asleep behind the camera. The eyes were dark and almost reptilian.

'That – I can't – it's a double exposure.'

Of course. That was the only thing that could make any sense of this. 'You've used the film already, then you've loaded it again, in your sleep. That's a used film, damaged.'

But he looked back through the other photographs, the same blur of grey. He took the magnifying glass out of her hand. Bent in towards the images. A person, but hunched over, like a wizened woman with a spinal scoliosis, arms, legs, and there in the last photo, crouching in the corner of the room, those large black eyes and he felt the cold creep down from his shoulders across his back as he remembered her, empty-eyed, running without seeing, pointing her camera towards a seemingly empty corner of the dining room, winding the film on, that familiar whir and click.

*

All evening they shuddered in the stray draughts. They had been living here for years and yet suddenly it all seemed unfamiliar.

'You're right. It is a double exposure,' Emily said. They had not mentioned the photographs for hours. They had been actively talking about other things, mostly the neighbours. How could they use a leaf blower when a broom would be fine? Why did they cut their grass so close that it looked like it was patchy and diseased? 'I'm sure I used that film. I don't know how I did it, but somehow I rewound it in my sleep.'

They fell into silence, both of their brows furrowed as they wondered about the mechanics of such a thing.

'Unless I exposed the paper and then put it back in the plastic. That's possible, right? If I'm taking photographs in my sleep, maybe I got the enlarger going and exposed the paper already and—'

The kettle shrieked and Emily let out a little startled cry.

'It's a double exposure,' Brendan told her, rubbing her shoulder reassuringly as he reached past her to turn the kettle off. He noticed the cold air trapped in that particular area of the kitchen. He flinched when a pile of dishes in the sink shifted, making a little clattering sound. They both sipped their tea slowly. After this cup it would be time for bed.

  KRISSY KNEEN

Brendan listened to her breathing. It had deepened, dropped into a rasp that was almost a snore, flattened out into these slow quiet breaths. Her eyes twitched. This was the REM sleep, the time for nightmares and somnambulists. He watched, unsettled, wondering what he would do if she were to rise up like the undead right now. She only shifted, turning onto her side and then the deep relaxed breathing continued.

He wouldn't sleep. He knew it. The house creaked at night. It always had, but now each floorboard stretching was an invisible footstep. Each gust of wind creeping under the door was the stale breath of nightmare. He closed his eyes and saw those other eyes, wide and round and dark as death, staring back at him, the hunched shoulders shivering from side to side, shaking as if it were an image on a television channel that had not been tuned in properly. The image shifted from side to side, a shudder of electronic unease. Possums on the roof could be something else entirely, wind in the trees a rustling of papery skin.

Brendan would not sleep. He opened his eyes and stared at the ceiling. His fingers were tangled in the sheet, his back was a clench of muscles. Fight or flight. He wondered, if it came down to it, which one he would choose.

*

He wakes with a start. It's happening. There is moisture on his cheek where his mouth was open in sleep, leaking spit onto his pillow. Asleep against the odds and now he is so suddenly awake and it is happening, here now. The sound of a shutter blinking, capturing an image, or not. The room is nothing but shadow. There is barely any moon, enough light through the blinds to throw a series of jagged slashes across her back so that she seems torn by the ragged claws of the moon. She is hunched over in a corner and there is that sound, that winding on of film, that whir and then a click. He feels his own heart racing too fast. He is sitting up in bed and doesn't remember how he came to be this way. The sound of blood pounding in his skull is too loud. It is muffling the whirr click, the possibility of other footsteps, the shuddering of leaves or shivery skin.

'Emily!' He means to shout it but it is just a strangled whisper. She doesn't seem to hear. She turns but not towards him. She holds her camera up pointing it at the bedside table, to where his book is perched, open and facedown to an unfinished chapter; to where the clock says three a.m.; to where the lamp crouches in darkness. The whirr. The snap. And then, perhaps a delayed reaction, she shifts slightly and she is looking directly at him.

At last. She sees him. Her eyes are focused on him. He begins to smile. The spell is broken, she is awake. He opens his mouth to say her name but all the air is pushed suddenly out of him and he is flat on his back, pinned. There is a weight, a terrible weight that shifts erratically from one side of his chest to the other like a small child stomping one foot then another on his rib cage. There is a shudder, but he is not sure if it is from the weight on his chest, the creature moving in a shiver as it did in the photograph, or just the embodiment of his own fear. He watches as she lifts her camera to her face, drags the winder across, a whir, focuses. Focuses on him. On his face. On his mouth that is suddenly closed, his nose, blocked, the suffocation of an invisible hand pressing down against his face.

Then Emily presses the shutter.

Brendan hears a final click.

***

Sealer's Cove

Chris Flynn

It must have been two in the morning but I had no real way of telling. It was a dark moon and when I looked back to the tree line I couldn't see our tent anymore. I only knew I was at the water's edge because I could feel the ocean lapping gently against my feet. It was one of those summer nights everyone complains about – the temperature had not dropped below twenty-five and I had left her in a fitful sleep, spreadeagled like a pale, sweating star on top of the pointless sleeping bag. The waves felt good around my thighs as I waded in to cool off.

Farther along the beach, down near the official campsite, I could see a pinpoint of light bobbing and weaving in the air. Someone with a torch was scanning the shoreline, maybe looking for shells or nocturnal creatures. I had heard turtles came ashore to lay their eggs here, but I had never seen any. I sank down into the water, washing away the sweat from my chest and tattooed arms, floating on my back amongst the gentle breakers as I tried to pick out constellations.

The light from the torch was coming closer to where I swam and the thought then occurred to me that it might be a park ranger. We could get a hefty fine for camping on the protected beach. There were signs everywhere stating that you had to stay within the boundaries of the official site, signs we had deliberately ignored in our desire to find a sandy spot where we could drink wine and hang out naked without incurring the judgement of others.

I stood up and slunk ashore, dripping and panicked. The beam of light was much closer than I had initially calculated. If I made a run for the tent, the movement might alert the ranger to its presence. We were so well hidden under the canopy I was sure the ranger wouldn't be able to spot it from the waterline, but he or she might see me. I had to hide.

My only option was to squat behind some rocks at the end of the beach and hope the ranger, if it even was a ranger, would turn back when they reached the headland. Like some water sprite I nimbly clambered over the rocks and folded my gangly wet limbs into a crouch, hugging my knees.

The figure stopped within ten metres of where I was hiding to look out to sea. It was a ranger all right, a man, keeping an eye out for those fabled turtles. I swore silently under my breath and then a laugh almost slipped out of me as I entertained the notion of leaping from my hiding place, roaring, to frighten him. My only concern was that he might have a heart attack, or club me to death with his torch in the assumption I was some ginger sea monster risen from the depths to terrorise campers.

I waited ten minutes behind the rocks, feeling like a primitive man come down to the sea to gather kelp or wash my matted hair. The ranger crouched by the water's edge and then sat down completely, settling in to survey the tides and contemplate some philosophical conundrum. He didn't seem to be in any hurry to leave, so I rose to a low stoop and carefully chose a path around the rocks without him noticing my departure, aided in no small way by it being an especially dark night. After a few minutes I was out of his line of sight completely, and quite enjoying myself. I had no idea what lay around the headland but figured I would be able to find an alternative route back to the tent, or at the very least just enjoy an unexpected nude stroll.

A welcome breeze wafted in from the sea and I turned my face into it, closing my eyes for a second to enjoy the sensation on my skin. When I opened them again I became aware of voices, and other, unidentifiable noises coming from the inlet just around the rocks. I ducked again and proceeded more carefully than before, thinking it would be just my luck to run into a party of campers staying up late to dance on the isolated beach, although at that late hour they would probably welcome a naked stranger.

No one was dancing. I stared dumbly at the scene for a moment before dropping to the sand in bewilderment. Cautiously, I peered over the lip of the rock to confirm what I had just glimpsed.

A three-masted sailing ship was anchored in the bay, not some shiny modern replica that toured the ports of the world to give sightseers a glimpse of yesteryear but a filthy-looking old hulk straight out of a pirate movie. The shoreline was abuzz with activity as men in ragged costumes were occupied skinning seals. A large pile of the dead animals lay at one end of the narrow beach and even in the darkness I could make out the stain of their collective blood on the sand as it seeped down to meet the sea.

     CHRIS FLYNN

I was in the process of trying to work out how scenes from a movie were being filmed so close to the campsite without anyone having mentioned it and wondering if Geoffrey Rush was out there somewhere when something cold and round and hard was firmly pressed into my neck, just behind my left ear.

'Stand up,' a voice growled. I did as I was told, modestly cupping my cock and balls in my hands. On-set security, I figured. This would be embarrassing. The barrel of whatever it was pressed insistently into my neck and I found myself shoved unceremoniously forwards out of my hiding place. I've never been much for respecting rent-a-cops and so I stepped quickly sideways and swatted at the weapon, turning as I did so.

'There's no need for that,' I said to the man, who, to my surprise, was dressed in full seafaring regalia. I only caught the look of irritation on his mug briefly, as out of the blue he swung what seemed to be the butt of a musket and cracked me on the temple with it. I wasn't knocked out but I did fall, my head ringing. I was about to shout, 'what the fuck' when he kicked me in the guts and all I could do was curl up in a protective ball. Two sets of hands picked me up by the armpits and dragged me along the sand to a campfire that was burning not far from the dead and dying seals. I was thrown roughly to the ground, my vision clouded from the whack on the head.

There was around thirty men going about their business on the beach, and no camera crews in sight. Most of the men were involved in cutting up the seals whilst a few others looked on. A separate group of four filthy, half-naked, wretched-looking women were in chains not far from where I lay and to my shock one of their number was being rudely assaulted by one of the mariners. Any doubts I still harboured that none of what I was witnessing was real were completely banished when I spotted what was jutting out of the man's pants.

'Jesus Christ,' I hissed, scrabbling back on all fours until I bumped into the legs of a man I had not seen standing behind me. He kicked me painfully in the ribs.

'Take it easy, you,' he muttered. 'Captain will deal with you when he's finished.'

I averted my eyes from the horrifying spectacle, though it drew a few cheers from the other men. Mercifully, it was all over quickly. The man buttoned up his britches and approached the campfire, sniffing and wiping his hands as if nothing had just happened. He jerked his bearded chin in my direction.

'Who's this?'

'Found him watching us from behind the rocks down there,' the man behind me answered.

The Captain nodded appreciatively. 'Escaped from Van Diemen's Land, did you? Done well to get this far. Suppose you must've eaten all your mates, eh?'

That elicited a round of laughter from the assembled men, who were now all watching me keenly. I made a snap decision to play along with whatever was happening.

'Well I'm not hungry, if that's what you mean.'

As the sealers all guffawed, I realised that with the beard I had spent the year growing and the sleeve tatts, all I needed were a three-pointed hat and a cutlass, and I'd fit right in with this motley crew. The man they referred to as 'Captain' punched a nearby colleague on the shoulder.

'Get this cove some skins.'

As his burly associate departed, the Captain fished around in his jacket until he found a small, round bottle. Pulling the cork out with his blackened teeth, he approached and offered me a drink. I cautiously sniffed the foul-smelling unction before tipping it back and swallowing the liquor. It burned all the way down but I managed not to cough or exhibit too much displeasure. This seemed to please the Captain. I nodded thanks and handed the bottle back.

'Lucky you come upon us, boyo. Fella could wander round these shores for weeks and not spy nobody, end up dying of thirst or hunger or get speared by the natives.'

I was about to explain that there was a gift shop and café half a kilometre away but held my tongue.

'Lucky, yeah. How long are you and your ... crew planning on staying?'

'We'll be shipping out on the morning tide so get some kip. You'll be coming along with us.'

'Actually I have other plans, but thanks.'

'Were a statement of fact, not an offer.'

Before I could protest any further, the overweight fellow who had been dispatched to fetch me some skins returned bearing exactly that. He handed me down a pair of crude trunks,

CHRIS FLYNN

fashioned from the hide of a seal. They did not smell terribly inviting but it was either that or parade around in the buff all night so I slipped them on. They were a snug, if slimy, fit.

I was left to my own devices after that and so I wandered around the camp, meeting the steely gazes of men who looked like they had recently strangled someone. The seal-skinning operation was appalling and I truly could find no indication that I was in the early part of the twenty-first century anymore. No dream I ever had was so vivid and the bloody scab forming on my temple was absolutely real. I could not explain what had happened. All I could think of was that I would never again disobey a 'no camping on the beach' sign. I flopped back down next to the fire, my skull throbbing, unable to form a plan of action.

One of the women in fetters crawled sheepishly towards me. I sat up straight and fetched her a ladle of water from a nearby bucket when I saw how parched she was. She sipped at it eagerly and no one objected to my interacting with her. Underneath the layer of grime that smothered her face, she bore a remarkable resemblance to my girlfriend, who I presumed was dozing blissfully one beach and about two hundred years along. I noticed her staring at my tattoos.

'Never seen ink like that afore,' she whispered huskily. 'Is that s'posed to be a demon?'

I held out my forearm so she could see it more clearly. 'Uh, no, that's Batman.'

'The cove what founded Melbourne?'

I had to think about that one for a second. 'No, a different Batman.'

'Friend of yours?'

'I wish. If he were here now, we'd both be out of this mess, though with everything that's happened tonight, I wouldn't be at all surprised if he came around the rocks on a jetski any minute. The Batski, I suppose he'd call it.'

The woman frowned at me. 'Don't seem like you belongs here.'

'Understatement of the year.'

She shook her head then, hair hanging in greasy threads around her face. 'If you want my advice, you'd be best flitting out the way you come, mister. I've seen men pressganged into service with the Captain afore and you ain't exactly in for a pleasant few months, I'll tell you that for nothing.'

Instinctively I brushed the hair back from her cheek, causing her to flinch. It was eerie how much she looked like her. I dragged the entire pail of water across so she could drink her fill and wash herself a little.

'Thanks for your kindness,' she said grimly, biting her lip as she came to a decision. 'I'll distract the mate if you want to make a run for it.'

'How will you do that?'

'You don't want to know, but it might be your only chance. Least one of us gets away.'

Much as I wanted to help her escape too, I had no way of unlocking the shackles on her wrists and ankles. I thanked her and decided to take her advice. Most of the men had accepted and already dismissed my presence by that stage, and so I was able to make my way to the back of their group at the edge of the campfire. As per her promise, the woman enticed the most senior of the renegades towards her side of the camp, and those who remained followed behind him to watch the lurid display. Given the rest of the crew were still engaged in skinning seals, I seized the opportunity to well and truly leg it.

I was already at the rocks when the alarm was raised. I glanced over my shoulder to see several of the men charging after me, swords held aloft. I had a good head start on them though and no intention of slowing down. I barrelled into the rocks and leapt between them as nimbly as I could, marvelling at how much easier it was to navigate a path between sharp, wet stones with three nineteenth-century pirates at my heels. It only took a few moments to round the headland and come within sight of the main beach.

The park ranger was gone and as I jinked between the rocks I realised the voices behind me had also faded into silence. I risked stopping to look back. I could see nothing except the ocean and the night sky. I waited for a minute longer, hands on my knees as I caught my breath. The men did not appear. The pursuit was over.

I stood by the water's edge for a while, gingerly touching the wound on my head. We had some antiseptic and sticking plasters in the First Aid kit back in the car. I could sort that out in the morning, on our way out of there. She was sleeping exactly as I had left her, oblivious to the night's events, the door of the tent flapping gently in the warm breeze. I had no clue how I might

　　　　　　　　　CHRIS FLYNN

explain why I wanted to return home two days early, though as I rested my hands on my hips and felt the slick seal hide against the skin of my arse I realised that whatever story I came up with, it had better be a good one. Wriggling out of the slimy trunks, I ducked my head and crawled back into the tent. She did not stir, even when I pushed a lock of hair back off her cheek.

***

A Cure

Alexander Cothren

Located on the 47th floor of a Manhattan business tower, Empathy International's reception room was sleek and antiseptically modern. It could have served as a template for any number of businesses – including the accounting firm at which Alice worked – save for one differentiating feature: a wall-length screen on which there played a slideshow of starving children and rubbled cities, interspersed with action shots of Empathy International workers dressed in their trademark pink uniforms, handing out food and building plywood houses.

Alice ignored this display by turning on her MindFi and playing Sudoku at full vision. She had been avoiding tragedy ever since she had first become aware of her condition, and she would continue to do so until she was cured. It had not been easy. Whilst awaiting the date of today's clinical trial, Alice's self-imposed ban had left her feeling increasingly isolated, both from the happenings of the world, and from her own peer group – who hissed and whispered at each other to change the subject every time they saw her approaching. She had become unusually irritable; her husband noted that she was like 'a smoker going cold-turkey', and indeed she felt as though she was suffering from withdrawal, as her emotions piled up inside her without access to their usual outlet. Even now, as she fiddled about absent-mindedly with the numbers in her game, she was fighting a deep, ferocious urge to rip off her MindFi visor and gaze up at those giant images, letting their expertly-framed pathos overwhelm her.

It was something of a relief, therefore, when Alice heard her name called, and, removing her visor, observed a man in a grey business suit hailing her from an open doorway beside the reception desk. A slim, attractive woman – obviously the trial's previous patient – was exiting just as Alice was entering. With a start, Alice recognised her as Kathleen Chandlay, a fellow member of her suburban tennis club. Alice's greeting, however, was caught in her throat at the sight of Kathleen's expression, which had a disturbed, haunted aspect to it. And Kathleen passed her by without even a flicker of recognition. Alice's heart sank.

She could read only one meaning in her acquaintance's troubled appearance: the trial had been a failure. There was no cure.

*

She had been using one of Empathy International's online hosts, to experience the devastation of a hurricane-struck Jamaican slum, when the ad had popped up in the middle of her vision. In large, dark lettering it asked:

Have You Been Feeling Less?

Beneath this was the black-and-white image of an African boy suffering from kwashiorkor, a bloated stomach hanging burdensomely from his otherwise emaciated frame. The image remained long enough for the child's round, wet eyes to burn into the viewer's conscience, before fading away to be replaced by another block of text:

Empathy International is currently trialling an upgrade to the MindFi system that may help cure Compassion Fatigue. Feel again. Apply for trials at empathyinternational.com/curecf

The advertisement faded, returning Alice to the shredded, Caribbean landscape, where her host's relatives were picking through the debris of their former home. She logged off, suddenly sick at the sight of their desolation. The ad had exposed something she'd long felt, but had been reluctant to admit: she was numb again. For some time now, a fog had been creeping over her ability to empathise with her hosts, whom she called on daily to escort her through the tragedy of their lives. She had subconsciously tried to repel it by searching for the worst situations that the wars, disasters and calamities of the world could offer – by indulging in sensations so extreme they would surely stir even the insensate; but the fog had rolled obdurately on, and Alice found she could ignore it no longer.

*

She was ushered into a small, clean room that was entirely bare except for one piece of furniture: an ovoid, metal pod with an open lid revealing a bed large enough for one adult. The man, who had entered and shut the door behind her, broke into a smile at the note of panic in Alice's face.

'It's nothing to be concerned about,' he said. 'It helps us block out any external stimuli, allowing you to better focus on the updates to our system. Please, lie down and make yourself comfortable.'

Alice removed her shoes and lay down on the plush bedding. 'Have you been a technician here long?' she asked, trying to dispel the nervous fluttering of her heart with small talk.

'Oh, I'm no technician,' the man replied, with the same thin smile. 'I'm actually somewhat of a Luddite myself. No, my interest in this trial is purely psychological. Here, put this on.'

The man had put on a MindFi visor, and he now handed a matching model to Alice. She slipped the strap behind her head and adjusted it so that the visor's electrodes fitted snugly against those implanted just beneath her skin. 'So, you're a psychiatrist?' she asked.

'I'm going to shut the lid now,' he replied.

*

For a few moments, she floated in a void of perfect darkness, before the screen of the visor flashed to life, delivering her to the Empathy International homepage. 'Can you hear me?' asked the man's voice.

'Of course,' she replied, then realised that his voice had come, not through the thick lid of the pod, but through her visor's speakers.

'Good,' continued the man. 'Now I want you to choose any host you like. This update will work for any one of them. However, you'll only be able to experience one – there'll be no jumping around from one to another like you might normally do.'

Alice thought she detected a hint of scorn in the man's voice, but nonetheless did as instructed, using the cursor implanted in the tip of her tongue to scroll through the site's active hosts. The most popular hosts of the moment were slum-dwelling Jamaicans, who, having barely survived the hurricane, had recently been struck by a catastrophic earthquake. As compelling as that double disaster was, Alice kept scrolling, hoping to find a less extreme situation that would allow her to better judge the changes in the new upgrade. She stopped on the profile of Gabra Zerezghi, a young African woman listed as suffering from

       ALEXANDER COTHREN

extreme malnutrition. A flashing red dot showed that this host was currently experiencing extreme trauma. With a flick of her tongue against her teeth, Alice entered this host.

*

Famine, especially African famine, held a special place in Alice's heart. As a teenager, she had been lured in by the media coverage of just such a crisis. She and her girlfriends had spent an entire summer huddled around their laptops, equally repulsed and fascinated by the images of a strange, skeletal people who languished in the dust bowl of their alien landscape, afflicted by some invisible curse. Moved by pity, they had collectively sworn off clothes shopping for a month, and had managed to scrabble five hundred dollars together, donating the entire amount to the Empathy International famine relief fund. That moment – when a click of the mouse had sent their money spinning out into the world – had been a singularly empowering one for Alice. She felt as if she had gathered the horrors and sorrows of the world on the flat of her palm, and then crushed them effortlessly in a fist. The intoxication of that feeling had set off an endlessly recurring cycle that had been a feature of Alice's life ever since: pity begetting benevolence begetting empowerment – the satisfaction of this driving her to seek further sources of pity.

*

Alice's host was crying. Tactile replication allowed Alice to feel the hot tears as if they were streaming down her own face. Visual replication allowed Alice to see the source of her host's grief: a collection of human-shaped forms wrapped in tattered white cloths and laid in a long row upon the red earth – her host's eyes being particularly drawn to one bundle no larger than a loaf of bread. Meanwhile, auditory replication distinctly revealed the wild, sing-song wailing of the gathered mourners, whilst olfactory replication brought to Alice's brain a strange muddle of smoke, acrid sweat, and the sickly, fruit-sweet breath of starving bodies.

The replication of each of these senses was state-of-the-art; it was easy for Alice to imagine that she truly was Gabra Zerezghi, that she had been transported to the site of a makeshift funeral held in a barren desert half a world away. Except that this was a game Alice had played many, many times before, and there was nothing new – neither in the technology nor in the situation it presented – to excite her exhausted emotions. Not even the emotional replication – which allowed Alice to feel the sharp stab of her host's grief, the churning bitterness of her anger, and the cold lethargy of her despair – could stimulate her. Emotional replication had been the last, great change to the MindFi system, with subsequent updates only serving to refine the tricky process in which the chemical output of the host's brain was recorded and then replicated in the user. Although familiarity had now eroded its potency, it had been a revelation upon its release – it had, in fact, once cured Alice of the exact same condition from which she was currently suffering.

Within ten minutes or so of inhabiting her host, Alice was able to discern that there was nothing ground-breaking in this latest update – if, indeed, there was anything new at all. Or perhaps her condition was too far advanced, her senses too dulled, and she was simply unable to notice the changes. Either way, it was clear her participation in this trial had been a waste of time. Her thoughts moved away from the catastrophe before her and focused now on the drudgery of the cross-town commute ahead. Alice moved to unstrap her visor.

Her arms refused. They seemed to reject the commands of her brain, and after a quick internal struggle Alice discovered they were not alone in their mutiny; she was paralysed from the neck down. She started slapping her tongue against her teeth, harder and harder, but the screen was as unresponsive as her body. Horror stories of MindFi meltdowns had been ubiquitous in the system's prototype for years, but safety features had long ago dismissed those concerns. Could it be a glitch in the new update?

Alice screamed for help. She could feel the force of her cries grating the inside of her throat, but the actual sound was drowned out by the voices of the mourners, and seemed to echo back to her from somewhere in the distance of the flat, African landscape. There was no response from Alice's world. Why did the man not respond? How long before he would notice something was wrong, and Alice would be rescued?

As time passed, the tickle of the flies congregating in the wet orifices of her host's face began to drive Alice mad. Her host was

         ALEXANDER COTHREN

continually wracked with violent sobbing, and each contortion of her atrophied muscles and cracked skin brought Alice a buzz of replicated pain. Sensations that had before been bearable – the stench of the bodies, the wailing of the mourners, the burn of the desert air – seemed to extract from their new constancy an intensifying fuel.

The fog had lifted; Alice was battered by the physical sensations of her host, and besieged internally by her emotions. She struggled to cling to any sense of self and, eventually, she succumbed. At the moment of dusk, with the African sun reduced to an ember glowing on the lip of the horizon, some barrier in Alice collapsed, and her despair merged with that of her host, finding kinship in the hopelessness of their situations.

Then, whiteness, and a disembodied voice, which asked: 'What do you feel?'

***

Baby's First Words

Kathy Charles

Roger carried the kid in his arms towards the back seat of the Subaru. Annette stood tentatively in the front doorway, chewing nervously on the edge of her fingernail. The child wriggled impatiently, threatening to slip through his hands. He held on to her pink dress, squeezing the little body tightly, too tight. She struggled harder, defiant.

Stop fighting me. Stop fighting me for chrissakes.

'Are you sure it's alright?' Annette asked.

'Absolutely.'

'I normally wouldn't ask—'

No, of course you wouldn't. You would ask anyone but me. Her own bloody father.

'No worries,' Roger said cheerfully. 'It's what I'm here for.'

'It's just that Mum's sick with the flu, and I can't reschedule.'

Roger placed the kid carefully into the back seat. He strapped her in tight, made sure the belt wasn't twisted. He was a good father.

'I would have put her in day care if I'd had more notice,' Annette continued, 'but they were full and I really need this job—'

A job interview. Yeah, right. How stupid did she think he was?

'—and if I get it I can work from home so you wouldn't have to do this again.'

'No worries.'

'I just don't like asking you to take the day off work.'

'It's fine. I squared it with Mark. Really. It's all good.'

Annette attempted a smile. She looked down at the ground before looking with concern towards the car, mouth tense.

She doesn't want to give me the kid. She's thinking twice about it. Good. I want her to think hard about this. I want her to think about this for the rest of her life.

'So I'll be back in a couple of hours,' she said, the reluctance showing on her face. 'If you could have her back by one o'clock in time for her nap I'd really appreciate it.'

'No problem.'

She paused. 'Are you going to your mother's?'

'Yep.'

Another pause. 'Say hi to her for me, will ya?'

'Will do.'

Roger stared at Annette, the woman who'd stolen the last eight years of his life. He'd slaved his guts out for her and the kid, given them everything. Now, in just a few months, she would be his ex-wife.

'Well, we'll catch you later.'

Annette nodded. 'Yeah. Thanks again.'

'No worries.'

Roger strolled across the gravel driveway, the sun beating down on his head. The summers were getting hotter, the seasons longer, and when the bushfires arrived, as they did without fail every year, they burned with the ferocity of a thousand suns. Most days Roger thought the whole world was spinning wildly out of control. Nothing much made sense to him anymore. He slid into the front seat, winced as the hot metal of the seatbelt brushed against his bare leg.

'Ready for a day with Daddy, princess?'

His girl didn't make a sound, just looked at him with those dull, blank eyes. Roger peeled out of the driveway, kicking up dust and stones. He watched Annette in the rear-vision mirror as she lingered in the doorway, watching nervously after them. He smiled and waved goodbye. Annette didn't wave back.

Enjoy your day, Annette. Don't you worry about a thing...

Good old reliable Roger. Always around when Annette's in a jam, even now after all she had done to him. He was a good father, a good man. Blokes like him were a dying breed.

'Sorry, Jodie. Mummy can't look after you today. She has an appointment with another man's cock. Now, now Jodie, don't judge her. We all have our priorities.'

Roger turned on the radio and floored the accelerator, racing past the cop shop and the supermarket, the post office and the bank, barely even blinking as the turn-off to his Mum's house receded in the distance. Jodie stared out the window, kicking her legs against some unseen phantom. Roger tapped the steering wheel. *Downhearted ... broken dreams that never really start-ed, ye-aah.*

The phone vibrated on the dash. Mark, of course. Nosy bastard. Roger let it go to voicemail, waited a minute until the little envelope appeared.

'Look, Rog, it's Mark. Where are ya? Listen, I know you've been havin' a hard time lately, but you can't keep not showin' up like this. Gimme a call will ya? I'm not mad, mate. I just wanna know you're alright.'

Job interview my arse.

Why would the bitch need a job? Roger was paying for everything. No way any man was getting a fair shake if the family court had anything to do with it. It had been the most humiliating day of his life, standing in that courtroom like a common crim, when it was *her* who should have been on trial. *She* was the one who'd broken their marriage vows. *She* was the untrustworthy one, not him. It was a war against fathers. A bloody disgrace.

Roger stared into the sun, let the tiny pinpricks of light play havoc with his eyes. It had taken them three years to save a deposit for the house: a little white weatherboard number just a few clicks from her mother's house. Roger had spent a fortune on it, painting the outside, fixing the gutters, putting in a new bathroom. Now it was all hers, hers and *his*. A doctor, of course. She hadn't much liked being married to a bricklayer. Not fancy enough for a girl with a uni degree. He'd found them in bed together, something no man should have to see. Poor Jodie had been dumped with the neighbours so her mum could have it off with the local quack. Just like she was probably doing right now, going down on the doctor in his lunch break, acting like the town whore. Good riddance to her.

And I'm the bad parent 'cause I lost my temper. What man bloody wouldn't under those circumstances? The good doctor got off lightly. It could have been much worse for him. He's lucky I didn't knock his block off.

Annette had an absolute field day spreading that little story all over town, telling everyone what a psycho he was. No, not a psycho. She'd called him a *sociopath*. He'd only done what any normal bloke would've done: given the good doctor something to think about. The way Annette carried on, you'd think no bloke had ever given another a black eye before. Annette loved to label everyone with big, impressive words. Roger had 'borderline personality disorder'. Jodie had 'learning disabilities'. Just 'cause the kid wasn't talking yet. She'd even had the nerve to say it was his dope smoking that had made the kid slow. Annette always blamed everyone else for her problems. Well, he wasn't going to be around to cop that anymore. The good doctor could take the blame for everything now.

Roger peered at Jodie in the rear-vision mirror. She kicked her feet and smiled and watched the gnarled tree branches pass by outside her window. She'd always been such a good kid. So happy, regardless of what Annette thought about her 'learning difficulties'. She was barely even two years old; so what if she wasn't talking yet? Annette had wanted to put Jodie in a special program, but he wouldn't let her. No way any kid of his was going to be treated different, like she wasn't as good as everyone else. He'd had that all his life, had it from his mum, his dad, Annette, everyone he'd ever known. He'd wanted to protect Jodie from that kind of judgement, but now it was out of his hands. The courts had seen to that, too. First it would be special programs and psychologists and then one day Jodie was going to go to a school for retards and lunatics and everyone was going to treat her like a freak. That might have been alright by Annette, but it wasn't alright with him. He wasn't going to let it happen. He wasn't going to leave his child, his precious princess, with that monster. She'd be better off with him. There wasn't a doubt in his mind that this was the right thing to do, for him *and* for Jodie. Let the people keep making their judgements. They wouldn't be around to hear them anymore.

Roger pulled into a clearing a few metres off the road surrounded by towering eucalypts, the perfect place. They'd be sure to see the car from the highway once they started looking for it, but for now he had time. He shut off the engine and opened the door.

'One minute, princess.'

He went round the back of the car and opened the boot. Inside was a red tool chest. At least the court had let him have *that*, he thought bitterly. He bent down and opened the rusty catch.

He wasn't like those blokes who threw their kids off bridges. Not that he blamed those guys. If they'd married a bitch like Annette, they had their reasons. But he couldn't do it that way, all that space and air before the baby hit the water. This way, it would be nice and fast. She wouldn't know what hit her, and neither would he. It would be the simplest, most painless thing he had ever done in his life.

Roger closed the boot. In the distance a car approached. The bitumen shimmied and glistened in the heat. Roger opened the boot again, removed the spare tyre and plonked it down by the side of the road. The car was next to him now, slowing to a crawl, the driver leaning out the window.

'You alright, mate?'

Roger grunted as he stooped over the tyre. 'Yeah, fine. Just got a flat.'

'Need a hand with that?'

'Nah, she's right.'

The driver ran his eyes over the Subaru, saw Jodie sitting there in the back seat.

'You sure about that?'

Roger fixed him with a hard look. 'I think I can manage.'

The driver gave the car another once over.

He's lookin' for the flat, Roger thought. *He's lookin' for the flat and he's not seeing it...*

Roger busied himself with the tyre, setting it straight and rolling it towards the other side of the car, the side the bloke couldn't see. He bobbed down, started fiddling with the screws and grunted, waited for the car to leave.

Just mind your own business, mate. This has nothing to do with you...

Roger paused, his body rigid. The car idled beside his, contemplating its next move. Finally the engine revved, and after what seemed like an eternity the car slowly made its way down the road. Roger watched it go, let the relief wash over him.

He'll probably be on the news tonight. Probably think about this day for the rest of his life. What he could have done, what he should *have done.*

Roger couldn't help that. What business was it of his? We all had our lot in life. Things we had to take care of, shit we had to deal with like grown men. Roger wasn't one to shirk his responsibilities. He'd dealt with the good doctor like a man, and he'd deal with this situation the same way.

He got into the front seat and slammed the door closed. He opened the glove compartment, hands steady as a rock. The kid gurgled in the back seat, a thick saliva bubble growing on her tiny lower lip. He tipped two bullets from the small yellow box into his palm, loaded them into the chamber and snapped it shut.

Dad.

     KATHY CHARLES

Roger looked around. A flock of cockies sat silently on the phone lines, watching him from a safe distance. The wind rustled the eucalypts. Roger felt the weight of the gun in his hand, slid his finger through the trigger and turned around.

Daddy.

Jodie's eyes weren't so dull anymore. They were bright and alive, full of wonder. She peered at the gun curiously, looked right down the barrel. Roger blinked, felt the back of his t-shirt thicken with sweat. He aimed the gun.

Roger.

Roger's eyes widened. *Yeah?*

What are you doing?

Roger looked around.

You can talk.

Yes I can bloody talk. You knew that already.

Roger blinked. *Did I?*

Sure you did. You were the only one. Mum thinks I'm an absolute drongo.

Roger laughed. *Yeah.*

She's got no clue.

You said it.

A pause. *Dad, what are you doing?*

Roger looked guiltily down at the gun in his hand, the barrel aimed squarely between Jodie's eyes. The sweat ran down his arms and slickened his palms, making it hard to hold the damn thing straight. Best to come clean with her. She was a smart kid. She would understand.

Jodie, you know I have to do this. Your mother, she's not a good woman. All she cares about is herself. She's no kind of mother at all. You and I, we're better off without her. She doesn't deserve us.

You'll get no disagreement from me there. The woman's an absolute train wreck. Couldn't organise a piss-up in a brewery.

Roger laughed again. *Too right.*

Roger was pleased. His kid sure had a great sense of humour, just like him. A chip off the old block.

Jodie's demeanour turned serious.

Things have been hard for you, haven't they, Dad?

Roger sighed. *They have, love. They've been bloody hard.*

You always did what was best for us, and this is how she repays you. It's not fair. You're a good man. A good father. The best.

You really think so? You're not just sayin' that?

Would I lie to you?

I would hope not.

I just want to make sure you're not doing this just to, you know, get back at her?

Roger's mouth dropped. *How could you ask me that? Me? Your own bloody father?*

Hey, I'm with you. I know you've got your reasons. But you know Mum, the way she talks about you. She'll think you did this just to spite her.

She can think what she likes.

Another pause. *Okay, you best get on with it then.*

Roger's grip on the gun tightened, his resolve strengthening. He knew Jodie would understand. She was a good kid, a smart kid. They'd all been wrong about her, and he'd been right. It was just the evidence he needed to push forward with what needed to be done. He steadied, finger trembling on the trigger, and swallowed hard.

Because, you know, if you wanted to get back at her, I know a better way.

Roger exhaled, rested his head against the car seat. Goddamn, this was hard. He was exhausted. It was so hot in that damn car, stifling. But Jodie didn't seem to be feeling the heat. Jodie was cool as a cucumber.

A better way?

Jodie nodded. *No one knows Mum like you and I do. No one knows what she's really like. With you and me gone, she'll be able to tell any bloody yarn about us that she likes. Especially about you. Can you imagine how she'll spin this? She'll make you out to be a monster. No one will understand.*

I told you. I don't care about that.

I think you do.

Roger thought for a moment. *What are you suggesting?*

Maybe it would be good if I stuck around, you know, to keep an eye on things? You'll need someone to speak for you, Dad. You deserve that.

Roger was too exhausted to argue. He was sick of it all. He didn't want to go back to family court every time there was a drama, didn't want to see the good doctor every time he went

     KATHY CHARLES

back to the house, Annette looking at the doc the way she used to look at him. He couldn't stand it. How any good man could live in this type of world was beyond him.

I tried so hard. I did everything I could.

You did, Dad.

And it wasn't enough.

Don't say that.

Maybe it's for the best.

Come on, Dad. You look tired.

Roger sighed. His eyes shone. *I am.*

You're such a good dad. You've done so much for me.

I have.

Jodie smiled. *Let me do something for you.*

*

Three hours later the police found Roger's car where he had parked it among the eucalypts. Roger's body was facedown in the dirt, ants swarming angrily over his back, gun by his side. The car was empty. It took them a few minutes to find the toddler in the clearing. She was propped up against a tree, happy as Larry in the shade, chewing greedily on a rusk stick. The police officer scooped her up, rocking her gently.

'There we are, sweetheart,' he said, holding the child gingerly. 'Everything's going to be okay now.'

His partner trotted over, shaking his head sadly.

'A bloody tragedy.'

'You said it.'

They both looked at the girl, who returned their gaze, silent and watchful.

'If she'd crawled into the sun she'd have been burnt to a crisp by now. She's lucky to be alive.'

The police officer smiled, and Jodie returned the smile three-fold, all gummy and full of cheer.

'Yep. She's one smart cookie alright.'

***

Navigating

Helen Richardson

The day Lucy finally agreed to drive her daughters to the factory outlet shop was the day she came face to face with her own demise. She sat in the car in the driveway reading a book, waiting out the last-minute fussing in the house. Her youngest daughter, May, came out and climbed into the back seat, a waft of a tropical scent, maybe jasmine, accompanying her. 'Bree's texting someone,' she announced before Lucy could ask.

'Great,' Lucy said under her breath, trying to catch May's eye in the rear-view mirror to share her exasperation, but May stared resolutely out the window. Lately May had moved over to the Bree camp. Lucy pressed the horn in three short barks and fired up the sat nav, clipping it into its holder.

'What's the address?'

'What?' It was May's reflex answer to everything.

'The address of the place.'

'Oh.' She fiddled with her bag and pulled out her phone.

One good thing about her daughters always having their noses in screens was their willingness to help with anything that involved looking something up. May rattled off the number and the street, and Lucy punched it in.

Bree came out banging the front door and made her way towards the car just slowly enough to irritate her mother.

'Finally,' Lucy said as Bree arranged herself and her black tousled skirt on the seat next to May. Looking like a crow, Lucy thought, but in a nice way, she added to herself. She backed the car out of the drive.

'Drive to the highlighted route,' Kylie, the sat nav voice, instructed Lucy in a broad Australian accent. May and Bree had set that sat nav voice from a range of perfectly acceptable softly-spoken alternatives. They liked to poke fun at Kylie: 'Go down that *stroit*, Mum', and Lucy could never work out how to change it over to one of the others.

Lucy drove through the suburbs following the sat nav's instructions. Kylie eschewed the main roads and liked to take shortcuts through streets Lucy had never encountered before. She suspected Bree'd had a hand in fiddling with a setting that caused

     HELEN RICHARDSON

Kylie to favour backstreets, but Kylie always got there in the end, so Lucy put up with it.

She surreptitiously checked on her daughters in the rear-view. May alternated between staring blankly out the window and glancing down to try to see what Bree was looking at on her phone. Bree had her Amy Winehouse over-made-up eyes glued to her phone and every now and then gave a little laugh. At one of these May leant over to have a look and Bree half-turned her shoulder. 'Get away, you bogan'.

Once Lucy and May would have tried to turn this back on Bree: 'A bogong *moth*?' Lucy might have said. 'Better than being an emo, at least I can talk,' May might have added. But lately Lucy couldn't be bothered complaining when her daughters were rude. She wasn't going to be a nag; she hated the way she was put in that position. It used to be that she was the quick-witted one, the girls wouldn't have a comeback and they'd laugh at her jokes and she was flattered when they copied her. It was fun when they were a tight, fast-quipping team. Okay, that was probably what frightened their father off, squeezed him out until he found some less wise-cracking partner but, all the same, Lucy looked back on that time with fondness. And now, karma of karmas, she was the one squeezed out.

'Just send me the link, then,' May said, obviously overlooking the bogan comment.

Bree sighed but Lucy saw her poke at the screen of her phone.

Send me the link, Lucy screamed in her head. They're sitting next to each other for chrissakes. Soon May was smiling at something on her phone.

'Take the second exit at the roundabout and then turn left,' Kylie said. At least Kylie was still talking to her. Lucy drew her concentration back to her surroundings. She had absolutely no idea where they were. The California bungalow and tree-lined streets had given way to blonde brick seventies houses with unmown lawns and upended kids' plastic tricycles. Now they appeared to be in some kind of low-level industrial estate, full of anonymous warehouses and dusty she-oaks. Lucy knew the factory store was on the outskirts but this was ridiculous. Kylie was confident, though, she piped up to tell Lucy to continue another kilometre then to turn right on Rowan Avenue.

There was a disturbance in the back and Lucy risked turning around to look.

'What's going on?'

'Get it off me.' Bree shoved May's big beaded bag onto the floor.

'It was just going to be there for a second. I was getting something out,' May protested.

'So?' Bree tossed her dark hair but amazingly kept her eyes glued to her phone the whole time.

May gave her mother a quick glance but didn't appeal to her for support the way she used to, instead she looked away, rummaging in the bag at her feet.

'God,' Lucy said, turning back to the front, and then 'shit' as Kylie reminded her to make the right turn. She pressed on the brake causing cries of Mum and shit from the back. 'Sorry,' she said, screeching the tyres on the turn.

'Just as well I wasn't doing my eyes,' May said, taking out her make-up bag. 'You could have blinded me.'

'You would have only lost one, unless you were doing both eyes at the same time. I'd like to see that.' Bree smirked.

'Alright,' Lucy said.

'Follow Rowan Avenue for four hundred metres then turn left into Yewfield Crescent.'

'Are you sure you gave me the right address?' Lucy asked May but she had her mirror up and was fingering a yellow colour onto an eyelid. It was probably called burnished sunset or something like that but it made her look vaguely sick. Lucy had become used to the dark kohl around Bree's eyes and her pale face that she made even paler with powder, but May had looked so pretty with her blue eyes and hair that sat so nicely around her face without the help of any 'product'. Of course now she followed Bree's advice and had her hair straightened so that it hung down like strips of gold tinfoil, her fine eyelashes clagged up with brown mascara. Her girls didn't know how beautiful they were without all the so-called enhancements. She couldn't tell them that now; they'd run away embarrassed or roll their eyes. She had told them when they were younger, hadn't she? She wished she could remember that she definitely had.

'It's what the website said,' May garbled, rubbing gloss onto her lips.

Maybe the outlet was on some kind of farm. It was a long way out; that's why she'd put off taking May and Bree even though it was, in their words, 'like, so cheap', and had 'the best designer seconds'.

     HELEN RICHARDSON

'Continue three hundred metres down Yewfield Crescent then turn sharply right onto Commemorative Drive.'

'You can't be serious,' Lucy muttered as she negotiated the tricky manoeuvre. It looked like Kylie had directed her to some kind of estate. They drove through a gateway in a stone wall and up a pine-lined drive. The road had seen better days and was potholed and rutted.

'This better be a damn good shortcut.' Lucy raised her voice: 'Can either of you see this place we are supposed to be going to?'

'Maybe, if you hadn't driven us into a paddock,' Bree said in an annoyingly non-committal tone. Lucy doubted she'd even looked out the window.

'Mum, you don't think this is a cemetery, do you?' May had unbuckled her seatbelt and was leaning forward, arms over the back of the passenger seat.

'Put your seatbelt back on,' Lucy said but she glanced from side to side and could see the headstones of neglected graves. The tussocky grass was overgrown and yellow wildflowers peeked through here and there.

'She's in the right place if we have an accident,' Bree said drolly but she'd ditched the phone and was studying the view out the window.

'Turn left on Restful Way,' Kylie commanded.

'Check that address, May,' Lucy said. 'This can't be right.' But she turned left anyway onto a thin strip of asphalt that was no wider than a footpath. The car was shuddering now on the uneven surface.

'Cool,' Bree said. 'Look at that one. See the angel.' She'd wound down her window and was taking a photo with her phone. 'The tip of the wing's gone.' She craned her neck to get a look at the other side.

'May, please, the address,' Lucy said.

'I'm trying. It's too bumpy.'

'Turn left down Autumn Avenue.'

'Should I?'

'Go, Mum,' Bree said.

Lucy turned, slowing down to a crawl. They were on a dirt track now. 'We'll need a four-wheel drive soon.'

'What's that?' May and Bree were both leaning forward and pointing at something out the front windscreen. A small, white wrought-iron fence surrounded a lone headstone; the track was heading straight for it.

'In two hundred metres you will reach your destination,' Kylie intoned, as though she'd done nothing untoward.

'This is so cool,' Bree said.

'It's creepy. I don't like it,' May cried.

Bree put her arm around her sister. 'It's fun,' she said. Then to her mother: 'You're going to stop, aren't you?'

'Do I have a choice? It's our destination. Kylie must have had a brain snap.' The car rolled up to the grave and Lucy turned off the engine. 'Come on.' But before she unbuckled her seatbelt the girls had tumbled out of the car and run over to the white fence. May turned back towards Lucy with a hand over her mouth while Bree stepped over the fence and crouched down next to the headstone.

'What's up?' Lucy shouted, getting out of the driver's seat. And then she sensed the peacefulness of the place, just the sound of wind through grass and a magpie calling. They could've been in the Outback. May was still standing there with her hand over her mouth. Lucy walked over but she couldn't see the stone because Bree was crouched over it rubbing the surface with her sleeve. For once, one of Bree's black outfits looked completely appropriate.

May tapped Bree on the shoulder and the older girl rose so that they both faced Lucy.

'What's going on? Is this some kind of game? You're giving me the shivers,' Lucy said.

'It's not a game Mum, we didn't know anything about it.' May ran over, grabbed Lucy around the neck and burst into tears.

'What's wrong?' Lucy smiled nervously at Bree over May's shoulder. Bree shrugged and stepped aside. Then Lucy saw the inscription on the headstone. *Lucinda Brooke.*

'My God.' It was surreal seeing her own name. Then she read out the inscription: *Faithful mother and wife, forever at peace.* Well it can't mean me,' she said. 'I was hardly faithful.'

'Don't joke.' May tightened her clasp around Lucy.

'And that's not how we spell our surname,' Lucy added. A small point but she was so glad to see the extra 'e'.

'She was thirty-four, Mum,' Bree said. 'If you'd died then, May and me wouldn't have been born.'

'I'm so glad I could oblige you with my longevity,' Lucy quipped. But she would have liked to have time to think about what it all meant, sit down here and think about her life, but it didn't feel right to do that in front of the girls.

'I'm going to take a photo and send it to Dad,' Bree said. 'That'll shake him.'

'I doubt it,' Lucy said. 'He'll probably think you photoshopped it.'

Bree took the photo anyway and they all stood around looking down at the marble slab.

'Why is she out here on her own?' May asked with a choke in her voice.

'Her family might have moved away,' Lucy said.

May clasped Lucy around the waist. 'It's sad.'

'It's good luck, you know. To see your name on grave like that,' Bree stated.

Lucy suspected Bree had made that up but she gave her top marks for trying to cheer up May.

'Is it?' May wiped her eyes with a tissue. 'Do you think there's anyone dead with my name?'

'There must be,' Bree said. 'We could ask Kylie.'

Lucy felt May shiver again and she gave her an 'I'm here' squeeze.

'I guess the sat nav had some technical glitch,' Lucy said.

'Oh, Mum, the address.' May felt in her jean's pocket for her phone and held it out. Lucy looked at the tacky website for the factory shop. 'Autumn Avenue. There's an Auburn Avenue, it could be a typo. We could give Kylie another try.'

'I'd like to look around here,' Bree said. Her hair had come loose from its clips and was blowing around her face like a wreath. 'We could try to find some other Brooke graves. You know, her family.' She looked at Lucy. 'Can we?'

'Can we?' May chimed in. 'That would be so cool.'

'Sure,' Lucy said. To her amazement Bree didn't mock May for that 'cool' and both girls stayed by her side as they wandered amongst the headstones.

'I feel like I've got a new lease on life,' Lucy said.

'Just as long as you're not going to be born again,' Bree returned.

'That would be a dead loss,' May added.

'Hey, guys. I don't think you should be joking about my—'

'Mum,' they both said.

'I'm being deadly serious.'

'Mum!'

***

The Local

P. M. Newton

In the end they all come to the pub. The rainbow ones. The feral ones. The organic whole grain ones. The repent-for-the-end-is-nigh ones, the live-now-for-the-end-is-nigh ones. It starts when they slow down, turn their heads, take in the sign and have their own wasn't-there-a-song-about-this-place epiphany.

For a time they speed up again, leaving a guilty dust trail as they wind along the narrow road that climbs through the valley, following the arm of the river backwards, past the waterfalls, on into the cliffs, the shady steeps and deeps of the ranges.

None of them want to stop at the dingy little pub in a town that doesn't even have a store anymore. At the markets they hear the rumours about the one-room bar populated by a few rusted-on drinkers, and each day the same handful of utes held together by dust parked up on the grass verge confirm those rumours. And so they drive past. That pub is not the future they intend in the hinterland.

As time goes by slower and slower they pass, still under-whelmed by the low wooden building with the tin roof and the bullnose verandah shading the rectangular space of the open door; untempted by the hint of movement in the cool dim interior, right up until the day they turn in. They all find their breaking point, sooner or later; or rather the hinterland finds it for them.

Usually on a day such as this one. Late afternoon, the sun pinking the edges of storm clouds, healthy flesh around a purpling bruise.

The publican reaches down a tall glass and wipes it. Watches the little yellow tray-top crunch over the gravel driveway, come to rest against the white painted poles that mark out the car park. First timers always use the car park.

The engine, tinny in the silence, ticks like a cheap clock after the driver turns off the ignition.

It's the hairdresser from up past Burrapine.

All winter the publican had watched the little yellow ute on its daily journey, buzzing through the town at sparrow fart, returning in the dark. Worked at a salon up in Coffs, that was the word. Two hundred and thirty clicks round trip. Over the months the little truck had grown louder. The muffler untended, the duco beginning to dull.

She introduces herself – Isa – sits on a stool, orders lemon, lime and bitters.

The publican passes it over, polishes the glasses. Listens.

Isa, because that's what Cal calls her. Her mother had called her Isabella, her sisters called her Izzy, but Cal, Cal had called her Isa. Made her feel like an Egyptian goddess.

Like Isis, she explains.

The publican nods, notices the slide the story makes into past tense.

No goddesses up beyond Burrapine, the publican doesn't say. Just lantana, landslides and shonky crops of Mullumbimby Madness.

Might have some vodka in this one please?

The publican obliges, settles onto her stool, awaits the tale. They all turn in, eventually. They all tell their tale, in the end.

Three days after we moved in, Isa says, the kitchen roof blew off. Blew straight off. In one piece. Straight over our heads. Over the house. Landed on what was – is – going to be – our veggie patch. I'd never seen a storm like it. Never. The wind. It just came straight up the valley, like one of them air-force jets. I thought one had hit us, you know? At first. But then the thunder, my ears popped. My skin popped. I thought we were going to die.

But they hadn't.

Like muffled drums at a memorial, thunder rolls in the distance. North Arm, the publican guesses.

Weather up here's like that, the publican says, spreading out a bar mat for a beer than hasn't been made for thirty-odd years.

The valleys, the hills and ranges, create these little eco-systems. Humidity rises, you get these storm cells, super cells – grow out of the rainforest – you can watch them, sit and watch the trees breathe out clouds, up they go all morning and then they charge about creating havoc all afternoon.

Some mornings the publican sits on the side verandah and watches the water fly up, fly up and about, building clouds the size of mountains, big white flat-topped anvils that darken before they avalanche back down in the afternoons.

Welcome to the hinterland, she says to the hairdresser, tops her up without being asked.

The hairdresser gazes down into her glass; a tear balls on her smudged eye-liner before it loses its balance, drags a trail of black down her cheek.

The publican pulls two schooners and a middy of shandy. Deposits one schooner in front of the grey-haired woman on a stool beside the pie-warmer. She doesn't look up, circling her picks in the form guide, transistor radio mashed up against one ear. The second schooner and the shandy go to the elderly twin brothers sharing the bench along the side wall. They sit beneath the jagged smile of the two-man saw, eyes resting on the clock above the bar that hasn't worked in the publican's memory. Out on the verandah in the gathering dark two old banana men nurse their beers and aching bones, voices low as cattle bedding down for the night in deep straw.

The publican isn't a local, thirty years not long enough to qualify. Need to be born here. That's how the locals divvied up the world. But with the banana plantations succumbing to lantana and their owners succumbing to old age, she might soon be the last one standing. At eighty, the Hurley twins still work their dairy, know all their girls by name, but pushing seventy these days the banana men talk more about selling up and hitting the road, joining the grey nomads to travel further north. Pat the Punter would probably die on her perch, the publican reckons, right under the fly-specked photo of the day her grandfather's bullock team hauled a trunk of cedar the size of house past this very pub, its verandah filled with pale women in too hot frocks.

The publican chews an ice cube, while the scent of jasmine gusts through the open doors. Like most of the blow-ins, she'd trekked north, drawn by the promise of Eden, communes, mud bricks and as much dope as you could grow. Five months later, when the rains caved in the adobe dome and her husband proved more useful at smoking dope than growing it or any other crop, she'd looked around for a wage. The pub had needed a bar useful and two years later, when her failed plantation king went into the rainforest and never came back out, she'd traded up.

The way the fresh young couple from Cronulla had eyed the melted mud-brick mound she showed them spoke of enthusiasm untempered by experience. She'd taken their money and a

P. M. NEWTON

new mortgage and bought the pub. The old owners, fourth generation, took off to Caloundra without a backward glance.

Touch and go there for a while after. For a year or two the locals looked betrayed, like a cattle dog that'd been kicked. With the closest pub forty ks away their choices were limited so, comforted by the publican's disinterest in making any changes at all, they stopped sulking and slipped back into the stupor of long hot afternoons cradling beers on the verandah, rehashing worn-out words, falling silent when a stranger wandered in.

The pub's minor claim to fame, being the subject of an old song that declared it had no beer, encourages a few visitors to make the potholed drive from the highway. But they generally fail to hide their disappointment at what they find: faded souvenir tea towels, coldy-holders and an uncharismatic clientele.

A cry from Pat the Punter makes Isa jump, as if only just reminded she's not alone.

Doggies, says the publican, taking Isa's money and supplying a third drink. Dapto.

But Isa shows no interest in Pat's fantasy quinella at long odds, stuck in the afternoon when the hinterland rose up to swipe her.

The kitchen looked like something out of *The Exorcist*, Isa says. The rain just poured in, all the dirt and muck and shit in the ceiling running down the walls, it looked like blood, like there'd been a bloody massacre in there.

She drains the glass, fingers scissoring for spare change in her bag.

It's not just the ecosystems brings the storms, you know. It's the rocks, the ores and metals in the rocks – acts like a giant magnet, draws in the storms, the lightning, all the forces – the energies.

A new voice.

Isa swivels on her bar stool, follows the publican's line of sight, back into the shadows in the far corner. The voice continues.

You know how many lightning strikes there are up here compared to the other valleys? And lightning's not all they attract. There's more. Seen it.

A pair of filthy feet in sandals, toenails long and stiff with dirt, jut out from beyond the massive jukebox; a relic from another age, dusty and dull, its coin slot jammed with a bottle top.

Dan here has his own ideas about the weather, the publican acknowledges, inspecting the man through the lens of a pristine middy glass.

All hair and tie-dye, beard and beads, he leans forward into the light. The movement of his arms as he demonstrates the summoning energies that draw the lightning is enough to release a wave of aromas, a mix of spice shop and op-shop, toe jam and bong water.

Isa stops searching her bag, nods to the publican, retreats back to her truck.

The muffler rips into the night. The publican listens to the engine straining up the hill out of town, the change in timbre when the gear shifts to tackle the climb past the dairy, the whine along the ridge, the twist at the top, falling in the drop down towards the bridge, growing fainter until it's only an impression, an eddy in the air, swallowed up by thunder leaping at the North Arm ridgeline.

The publican pulls Dan another beer and wipes down the bench tops. A flash fills the doorways, sheets through the bar. The phone gives a frightened trill and on cue the jukebox lights up and a plastic sounding guitar, distant and distorted, starts strumming.

Bottle top stuck in the damned thing ever since the publican began to work here. And in all that time she'd only ever heard it play that one song.

By the time the first verse finishes the rain is drumming on the tin roof, masking the sounds from the lips of the pub patrons as they join in on the chorus.

*

The roof had just been the start of their disasters, although at first it had seemed to have a silver lining. Neighbours, most of whom Isa and Cal did not know, turned up the next day and a working bee had the roof off the ground and lashed back onto the beams before nightfall.

Then a bonfire of broken wood. Beers and joints circling the flame, sharing hands and lips and intimacy under diamond hard stars.

            P. M. NEWTON

Isa remembers she'd felt happy that night. The roof back where it should be. Cal's arms around her, warming her in the chill of the hinterland night.

She parks the yellow tray-top and steps out into the burnt circle of grass. A day of cutting, curling, washing, tinting, blow-waving, chatting with feigned interest about her clients' weddings, anniversaries and frocks, now home to find the house in darkness, the chooks un-fed, un-watered, wandering around the yard, happy meals for local dogs.

The thunder had turned nasty on the drive home; she jumps as it cracks without warning. Her nostrils prickle with ozone.

It'd all felt possible that night. Joint-fuelled talk full of dreams and plans for organic veggies; a tractor could be borrowed from here to break up that river flat, a post-hole digger from there to fence a paddock, maybe plant an orchard of lychees, dragonfruit, rambutans and other exotics. Fruit bats had thumped the air as they passed overhead, as if eavesdropping, taking notes on a place they might revisit.

But the next morning, sandpaper tongue and sledgehammer headache, Isa walked into a kitchen that was still a scene from a nightmare.

And two weeks later it still was. The walls streaked with filth. Cleaning and repainting, that had been Cal's job. This time she hadn't cried, she'd yelled.

Their first big argument.

Isa shuts and latches the door to the hen house, too big now for the few hens left. The mutter and flutter of the girls settling in loosens something inside her; it takes a moment for her to identify it. Envy. She's standing in the dark at the end of a dirt road feeling envious of the companionship of a bunch of chooks.

She looks up. No stars. A flash of lightning from over North Arm glows like a distant city. It dies, leaving the darkness of the forest absolute.

She'd been naked, in their bed back in Sydney, Bronte beach, the morning air pinched with salt. She could taste it. Cal spread the map out across her body, his finger tracing the outline of their dream. The boundary of river, road and forest; her thighs, belly and breasts.

The Mistake State Forest.

What kind of name is that? Howling with laughter, rolling over mountains and streams, inking their skin with the print of topographic rings.

She shuts the front door. Fingers pause over the bolt before she drives it home.

Fuck Cal, wherever the fuck he is. Could be spinning out in the flotation tank down the hill at Thumb Creek or maybe over in Darkwood, drinking his own weight in home brew as payment for a day humping fertiliser up into that old bikie's crop site.

Isa doesn't bother turning on the lights. The storm plays silly buggers with the electricity anyway. Better to stay in the dark than have a whack of thunder and light snuff it out. She turns on the radiator, still chilly up here in early spring, and at least the orange glow dies slowly if the power goes, no terrifying plunge to darkness.

The room alternately floods with light then shadow as the storm leaps the ridge from North Arm and muscles up the valley. She pulls a crocheted blanket around her. She misses the cats. The dog.

The roof had been the first disaster.

There'd also been the tractor, borrowed for a day; Cal leaping off as it rolled end over end down the hill, big stupid Tonka toy wheels still spinning when it landed in the river. Then the neighbour who'd lent it to them, with his tight-lipped acknowledgement of good fortune that Cal had avoided being crushed followed by the halting demands for compensation they couldn't afford.

She'd wondered if it had been a sign. Like the snake. Coming home to find the kittens all dead, the mother cat dying, pulpy when Isa picked her up, the blood haemorrhaging beneath the skin.

The night Cal, drunk, came up the driveway and ran over the dog. The terrible howls that it took him three shots to silence.

And now, one by one, the chickens. From eight, to six, then five. Tonight she'd counted four. Tomorrow she'll find the blood and feathers.

Wind drives the rain up the valley, their house built right where it shouldn't have been, on top of a ridge, unprotected, assailed on all sides. The rain hits with diagonal force. She stirs and makes herself check all the windows. Fights with the wooden sash in the bedroom for long enough to soak her t-shirt before she gets it shut. She dumps the shirt on the floor, slides it around the puddles with her foot, abandons it soaking in the largest.

The storm toys with the kitchen roof. A flap, flap, flap of something loosening draws her into the doorway, a dark stain left over from the last rain now shines freshly wet as lightning paints the walls. She turns her back on the room, returns to the couch, the radiator dull and cold.

Camouflaged by the rattle of branches and leaves, it takes a while before she connects the rhythmic knocking at the front door to a non-storm sound.

She pulls the rug around her, opens the door a crack.

She smells him before she recognises him. Spices and smoke and dirt.

Dan from the pub.

She opens the door. Country etiquette demands it. The offer of shelter from the storm, though he seems almost dry.

He offers a greeting, hands pressed together like a monk. Bows, murmurs something that could be a foreign language or fluent bullshit. He slips off his sandals, although his feet are no cleaner, and sits lotus style on the floor. An orange glow bathes him.

The radiator returning to life.

He rolls a joint, hands it over, rolls another, produces flame from something small and shiny and silver, and they smoke in silence until Isa begins to speak.

When she wakes it's daylight; she's still on the couch, crocheted rug tucked around her, and the only sign of her visitor a pile of roaches in the ashtray and the faint smell of dirty feet and sweet weed.

*

A stormy summer. Stormier even than usual. All the banana plantations along Upper Taylor's Arm wiped out in a landslip. The publican's regulars dip when the two old growers take the insurance money and join the grey nomads heading to FNQ. The twin brothers lose five of their girls to swamp cancers when it rains solidly for six weeks, but they milk on and drink silently each afternoon beneath the two-man saw that their great-great-uncles once used to clear all the cedar from Ebor to Yarrahapinni. Pat the Punter still punts but arthritis means she's had to give up the stool. She settles for a spot on the bench between the jukebox and Dan.

A car slows down on its way through town. The heads turn and take in the pub. The sign. The flash of recognition. That song! About the pub with no beer. The publican can almost hear the laughter as it revs and heads up into the valley. A new car. She doesn't recognise it.

A battered jeep comes down the valley, bumps into the car park. This one she knows.

Young couple. From Adelaide, with a plan to grow tropical fruits on the river flat, maybe goats on the slopes to knock down the blackberries and lantana. Bought the hairdresser's place up past Burrapine.

Isa had called in on her way out of town at the end of summer. Dropped off the keys to the house. A blank envelope. No message. Hadn't looked into the corner, past the jukebox, where a pair of filthy feet in dirtier sandals stuck out.

She'd driven out of town without looking back.

A week later the publican had handed over the keys to the new couple and shouted them a beer. Answered their questions.

Yeah, cedar country back in the day – as they exclaim at the bullock team.

None left here now – as they touch the teeth of the two-man saw.

And the previous owners?

Split up.

Well, it was close enough to the truth. The publican had seen no point in going into the grisly details.

It was a lightning strike that had got him in the end, up in the Diehappy State Forest. From all reports the cops had had trouble keeping a straight face when they came to tell Isa.

Big old tallowwood, hit and split and left to die, had given up the ghost just as Cal was carting a length of poly pipe up to the old bikie's crop site. Half the trunk sheared off, fell, squashed him like a bug.

Isa had reported him missing, but to be honest, no one had really been that bothered to look. By the time Dan stumbled across him the only thing showing was a leg bone poking out beneath the dead timber, well gnawed by feral pigs.

The couple from Adelaide park the jeep.

They like the pub, they say. Want to be locals, they explain.

The publican decides to give them another month before she commits their names to memory.

P. M. NEWTON

The woman takes a seat on the side verandah. The man orders two schooners.

Dan's sandals slap up the wooden steps and the order is increased by one.

They sit, one either side of Dan, on the long verandah bench.

The publican leans against the doorjamb; watches the clouds build up over the range. Listens.

Dan tells them about the storms. About the metals and the ores. About the energies. About what it summons.

The couple from Adelaide pass a joint, nod and look up towards the hills.

He tells them about the night he was driving home and he saw the lights.

Dangerous Dan.

The publican had laughed when someone had pointed him out to her. Thirty years ago now, Bellingen markets.

Dangerous Dan, the Spaceship Man.

Thunder unfurls somewhere far away. A shift in the air, an almost subliminal glint of light.

The jukebox starts to play the only song it knows. The publican's lips begin to move along with Bowie's and from the side verandah two new voices join in. They hit the chorus of 'Starman' together.

***

The Koala Motel

Rhys Tate

Jillian called Dean before Ron was due to arrive that evening, and they talked through the past eighteen months of happenings. Then she said, 'Nothing serious but keep an eye on Ron, will you? He's drinking a lot more.'

'Than usual?' Dean replied.

'Since he took off for Birdsville. He's been shook up about something for months now.'

Dean coiled the phone cord around his oil-stained finger. 'Well, have you tried asking him?'

'I'm his wife, Dean. He's not going to tell me about it.'

'And I suppose—'

'Look, I don't need to know about it. Would I like to know? Yes, of course I would. Our marriage is a peculiar thing, but you have to understand that I still care very deeply for him. And I know when he's bottling something up. I don't care what it is, or who he tells it to, but he needs to let it out of his head. He needs to slow down and uncork a little.'

Dean sighed and gazed past a lost bogong battering itself silly against his kitchen window to the last shreds of pink in the western sky. He'd left the light on in the workshop again. It wasn't the first time that Jill had asked him to do something like this. 'Yeah, if the opportunity arises, I'll get on it.'

'You're a good man, Dean Donnelly.'

He smiled despite himself. 'Just don't go telling too many people.'

*

Ron arrived an hour later, his canvas trucking bag over his shoulder and a case of stubbies under one sunburnt arm. He put the case onto the kitchen table and slung his bag on the floor and the men grasped each other's hand, then Ron drew in closer and clapped his left hand on Dean's shoulder. Up close, Ron's eyes were bloodshot and the skin around them dark and puffy. Three bottles were already missing from the sweating case. Dean thought of the distance between the bottleshop and his house and what that meant. 'You still driving that bucket?'

'Nope, got a whole new bucket parked there in your driveway. Had it, oh, eighteen months now. Actually, you mind hoisting it up tomorrow morning? New set of brakepads to chuck on.'

They talked and Dean basted a splayed chicken roasting in the oven while Ron steadily ground his way through the first half of the case. His face was lutescent under the kitchen globe. Sometime after dinner, the conversation slowed and Ron asked him if he had anything stronger in the house.

'Stronger than a dozen stubbies?' Dean asked, already off his chair and reaching for the bottle of Scotch in his pantry.

'Geez, Mum, you've had … what?'

'I'm on my fourth.'

'So we got church in the morning or something?'

Dean poured them nips of Scotch into old Vegemite jars. Ron flipped his back and then held out the jar while Dean ran another measure into it. Ron winked and Dean chuckled softly and shook his head. He sat and they both sipped. It was time.

'Seems like you've been hauling some heavy thoughts in that big old head of yours,' Dean said.

Ron rocked back on his chair and stared at the ceiling for a moment. 'When did she call?'

'Today. But I don't need Jill to tell me. You look like shit, mate.'

'Yeah, well.'

'Only that I've known you a long time. And vice versa. So if you've got something to let fly, you know it's going to stay right here in this kitchen.' They were silent for a while and then Ron farted thunderously. The men looked at each other and then folded forward as the breath wheezed out of them.

Ron wiped his eyes, and then his face changed. He swallowed. Dean could almost see the knot of words in his throat. 'I don't even know where to begin with this.'

'Try at the start. Usually works for me.'

'Look, yeah, but—'

'Just spit it out, will you?'

For a moment, there was just the rhythmic tink of the moth against the kitchen window, as if it was also waiting for Ron to finally speak. 'Alright. Alright. So, nearly a year back I was out in the middle of nowhere along the wheat belt, in the Toyota outside, loaded up with supplies and my best suit, heading to a wedding out at Birdsville. Mad Mick's wedding, actually. You remember Mick? Hell of a place to hold a wedding. Anyhow, on the way there's a spot out there between Pinnaroo and Loxton where this couple once set up a motel. The Koala Motel, they called it. There was a small lake nearby fed by a strong underground spring. Lots of eucalypts, and where you get a lot of those, you know you get koalas coming in to feed. They built their hotel and sunk a well to get enough water for the people who stayed. Good water, too. Clean and sweet. And, for a while, they came to stay. You could fish the lake there. Great fishing, people said.

'Something went wrong with the water, though. The well they sunk turned sour. Didn't matter how many times they changed the filters on the pumps, people came out of the showers smelling wrong. Faint smell, but bad, like they'd swum downstream from a drowned sheep that'd been floating there for a month. Muddy and rotten. Then, over the course of a year, the spring dried up, just out of the blue. With the spring gone, the lake started going as well. Just the deeper bits near the middle. The trees died off through a couple of those long, hot summers and the koalas packed up for better places. And with all that gone, there wasn't much reason anymore for people to stay at the Koala Motel.

'The bloke and his wife should have packed up with the koalas, but they had sunk too much money into the place to just walk away. They tried to bore fresh wells at the motel, and more out near the lake bed to see if they could pump water up to fill it.Which is as mad as it sounds, like trying to refill a swimming pool with a teacup. There was a bore crew with a post rammer out in the scrub, hammering the ground and measuring that with long drill electrodes. Got funny readings, they said. I mean, there are holes everywhere in the limestone and sandstone and some caves even older, but they got bad results beyond that. Where the signals showed aquifer, they'd just turn up dead, dry rock, or water tainted with sulphur and God knows what.

'At the end of the drilling the couple went bust, surrounded by dry wells and bills coming from everywhere. But then, the worst thing happened. Their little boy vanished one afternoon. The lad must've been about four or five. The news latched on to the story for a while, and the photo they used for the missing

　　　　　　　RHYS TATE

posters still sticks in my mind – blond hair, sitting on his little blue BMX pushbike, squinting into the sunlight behind the photographer, the motel in the background.

'The last they saw him, he was riding his bike in circles in the shadows of the empty parking lot at the front of the motel. His mother was doing paperwork in the office, keeping half an eye on him through a window while she shuffled the bills into piles. When the police came, she told them she was certain that nobody had stopped at the motel when he disappeared. By that point, the couple were so desperate that one or both of them would come running out if they heard a car even slowing down on the way past.

'But you know what young fellas are like. Get an idea in their head for exploring and off they go. And off he went, into that lengthening afternoon, and was never seen again. Him or his bike. Just tyre tracks in the sand which led away from the motel for a bit, until the wind blew them out.

'Course, the first thing they thought was he'd fallen down one of the old mines in the area, dug around the same time that they struck opals over in Mintabie, 'cept all they ever found around Pinnaroo way were milk opals. The contractors had the mines they found fenced off with star pickets and that orange barrier tape, but some of it had already been torn away, by animals or people or whatever was out there. The police came in and lowered a spotlight down the drops and said that they were empty. Nothing in the bottom but that dry yellow rock, and the bones of things that had fallen in over the years and died staring up at the thin circle of light above them.

'But there was one of the opal mines, they said, that had no bottom they could see. They lowered the spotlight more than one hundred feet with the light shining off the walls of the mine, and once they passed a certain point, that reflection just went. Just the tiny spotlight, looking like a candle down there, and dark all around it, until they ran out of cable. Whoever'd been digging had broken through to an underground cave, something carved out of the rock thousands of years ago, the coppers reckoned. Those caves can be hundreds of feet deep. They never said this to the parents, but if the little fella had fallen down this one, he was there for good. No way to ever recover the body.

'Now, losing a child is a terrible thing, of course. The wife took it hard, though. Very hard. People said she kept hearing her son at night, crying in the distance. She and the husband would go out with six-volt torches, walking back and forth across that flat scrub, calling out to him. But they could never make out the direction of his cries. Just when they thought they were getting closer, the cries would start coming from somewhere more distant.

'Then, right when the bank was going to take the motel back, the pair of them just up and vanished. Left their car behind, abandoned all their things and took off into the sunset with what they were wearing. Like that ship they found with a half-eaten breakfast laid out and the crew gone mid-bite. The bank tried to sell the Koala Motel, but no one was crazy enough to buy it. It just sat out there, getting trashed by the weather and the carloads of local kids who went out that far to throw parties the town jacks couldn't bust. By the time I was due to drive past, ten years down the track, the Koala Motel was a sorry sight. All the windows gone, the doors to the rooms kicked in, holes in the roof.

'I was about half a kilometre from the motel, passing the dried-up lake bed and all the dead, twisted gums, when the radio flared up for a moment, loud and distorted, like someone had ripped both the dials clockwise. I was reaching for it when there was a flash of white across the road and I heard a thump under the ute. I pulled up and turned around to shine the headlights back along the road. Got out with the torch. Thought maybe I'd hit a wombat, and you know what one of them can do to the underside of a car. Tear the muffler right out from underneath you.

'There was nothing on the road or in the gravel, either. When I wheeled back around in the direction of Loxton, there was a grinding from under the ute, like a bearing had gone. Too right, I thought, miles from nowhere and no one else around. If I couldn't crawl under the ute and fix whatever was wrong with it, I was going to be stranded until morning.

'I limped it down the road until I could pull up in the parking lot of the old motel. It was a square lot, with the building running around three sides and the fourth open to the road. White brick walls and dark rectangles where the windows and doors used to be. Graffiti and broken glass everywhere. Smashed furniture dragged out under the stars. Mattresses and fire pits and drifts of weathered paper and plastic.

'I figured I could drive one side of the ute up onto a concrete gutter, which would give plenty of room to scoot underneath and take a gander at that bung bearing. Thing was, once I was under there with my torch, I couldn't see a thing wrong. Wheels and brakes were all fine, muffler in one piece, no oil leaks. I crawled back out and stood there, scratching my head, thinking over what could be causing the grinding. Turned my torch off to save the battery while I puzzled it through.

'That's when I heard the crying. It was soft at first, but over the course of about two minutes, it grew louder, like it was moving towards me. This thin, high-pitched sobbing from someone upset. Maybe some sort of animal? I stood there for a while, trying to work out the source, because the crying was bouncing off the motel's walls and coming in from every bloody angle.

'I was thinking, alright, maybe someone got dropped off here earlier as a prank, or was trying to squat out here, and was wandering around in that endless Outback dark with a massive case of the heebie-jeebies. I was getting a decent dose myself by then. *Oi!* I yelled. *Where are you? I'm here in the car park.* If they were lost, I could help them. I wasn't going to leave them floating around until daylight.

'Whoever it was gave one final holler, then went silent. I stood there for a minute, but that last cry sounded like it came from inside the reception area of the motel, smack-bang in the middle of the building.

'I rolled the ute off the gutter to point at the reception and left the headlights on full beam. Took the keys, of course. I wasn't planning on being there for any longer than a quick captain inside, because the last thing I wanted was to be stuck with a bung car and a flat battery.

'Inside was much as you'd expect it. All the windows kicked out, dry mould chewing at the carpet, the wood panelling on the walls bulging out where thunderstorms had come in through the roof. Beer bottles with faded labels in the corners. My shadow creeping across the wall from the headlights behind me.

'Beyond the reception was another room. The door to it had been ripped off its hinges and thrown on the ground, and I had to walk over it to peer inside. Of course, not so much of the light from the ute was getting past me into here, but I had my torch. It looked like a storage area. There were deep shelves either side and a few stained blankets and sheets balled up on the floor. I could see another room beyond this. The door to this room had a circle cut out of it, with a perspex window installed. I shone my torch through. The perspex was scratched and yellowed, but beyond the door was a large kitchen, with stainless steel splashbacks and an industrial stove tipped onto its front.

'I pushed the door back and propped it back with a three legged chair. *Anyone there?* I yelled again. Silence. *Someone playing funny buggers?* Right, stuff this for a game of soldiers, I thought, turned around and walked back outside.

'I'd just opened the ute's door when the crying started again. It was clearer this time, and I could tell it was definitely coming from inside the motel. I walked back in, the cries amping up. Only, this time there seemed to be something wrong with the sound. I stopped and thought about that for a moment, but I couldn't work it out.

'It was only later that I realised why I stopped. The crying had a pattern. I can still hear it, the sobs and hitches in the same places, like the crying was on a tape that looped every five or six seconds. As if it was a recording. Or something imitating a sound it had heard. Lyrebirds do that ... they pick up the sound of things around them and then call it back, note-perfect. Hear them imitate a car alarm or a power drill and you'd think that's what they were. But that sound is just an imitation. That's all it is.

'I was getting angry now. Someone was playing a prank, alright, and they were playing it on me. The crying was coming from the kitchen, and I shone my light around. At the far side of the kitchen, I could see a set of steps which led down to another room.

'Some places out here are built like that. They dig a kind of basement cellar, to keep food and wine at a steady temperature over summer. I stepped around the overturned stove and shone my torch across the steps. It was a big space down there. The crying was very loud, echoing up the stairwell, and there was a smell too – old and damp, and something else I couldn't put my finger on. Like spice that had gone rancid and sour. At the base of the steps, I could see smashed jars

  RHYS TATE

and rusty tins, and the bones of a fair-sized animal. Maybe a feral pig had nosed its way into the kitchen, attracted by the smell, then busted a leg on the way down there, become trapped, and starved. But even as I was thinking that, I was thinking about how none of it really made sense.

'*Oi*, I yelled for a third time. *Joke's over. You can come out of there right now.*

'The crying stopped in an instant. An echo for a moment or two, and then nothing. Just that smell. I had a dog that died at home, once. Remember Bear? Went off his tucker for a couple of days and died before I could think about taking him to the vet, poor fella. That was what the smell was like. Sick, musty dog. And I realised that I could hear something, after all. A measured breathing, just out of the range of the torchlight.

'Now, you can say that a person can breathe heavily, but this wasn't like that. Anyone who's worked around animals will tell you that big things come with lungs of a similar proportion. And whatever was down there sounded damn big. Just me, and the breathing, and then bang, the crying started up, but twice as loud. And different again. Not just the cries of a child but another set of cries matching it and the hoarse bellowing of a man in pain over the top.

'I didn't stick around to see what it was. No bloody how. Not with my ticker trying to punch a hole through my shirt. I backed my way out of the kitchen double-time, nearly tripping over that bloody stove on the way. I reckon whatever it was, it didn't like the light at all. Maybe it had lived all its life somewhere deep down in the dark, and then found its way up to the surface. To us.

'Say I did trip over and dropped the torch? You know how torches fall to pieces when they're dropped, even the good ones, and all I had was a taped-up Dolphin. If there was no light in that kitchen? I reckon whatever it was would have been up those stairs and onto me about two shakes later.

'I backed out of that motel to the ute, then I backed the ute out to the road, and then I gave it a fair hammering until I hit the streetlights at Loxton.

'If I blew it up along the way, so be it. But the thing was, that noise under the ute went soon after I took off. I had a proper look under it in the morning, and there was nothing wrong. Clean as a whistle.

'Bloke I know in Loxton told me that someone set fire to the motel a couple of months later and the council finally got off their freckles and bulldozed what was left into the basement. Got funding to seal those old mines with concrete caps. And that was it. All she wrote. I've thought long and hard through what happened. Can't stop thinking about it. And I can't work it out at all.'

There was silence. Dean nodded, staring out of the window at the bogongs tapping against the glass. He'd known Ron, a bloke as grounded as a lightning rod, since they weren't much older than the missing boy. Finally, he said, 'You fair dinkum?'

'Fair as a May rose.'

Dean poured them another nip, searching for the right thing to say. Ron seemed to be out of words. They both sipped and then Dean said, 'Something like that's got to disturb your way of thinking about the world.'

'I wouldn't say disturb, exactly. But I'm definitely a decent way from feeling turbed about the matter.'

*

Early the next morning, Dean had Ron's dusty Toyota up in his workshop's hydraulic hoist. Ron eventually staggered out of the back door and scrubbed his eyes in the sunlight. He limped into the workshop and winced as Dean let a spanner ring off the stained concrete floor.

'So we've well and truly missed morning service,' Dean said.

'Geez, I thought you were joking.'

'Course I am. Thought you were going to give me a hand with the brakepads, though.'

'Yeah. Got a bit carried away, didn't I?'

'You turned one on, for sure. Can you get this wheel off for me?'

Ron huffed and grunted as he lifted the wheel away from the studs and set it on the stained concrete. 'About that ... I might have said some things last night.'

'I reckon you did.'

'Just ignore it, alright? Load of piss talk.'

'Maybe.'

'So, what, you believe what I said?'

'I believe you heard what you heard out there and that's good enough for me. Maybe there's a better explanation, I don't know. But I know you'll go bonkers thinking too long about something like that.' Dean frowned. Now the front wheel was off, he could see that there was something wedged deep in the ute's suspension, caked with road grime. He took a long screwdriver from his tool belt and worried at it.

'Unless I'm bonkers already. Now you've got a great story about how Ron Whitmore's finally lost his lollybag.'

'What did I say last night?' The object dropped out of the suspension spring. Dean caught it as it fell and wiped a fingers' length of the oily dirt away. A wonky, scarred trapezoid of metal with blue plastic and paint peeling off it and a chrome rod running through the centre that had been bent back and snapped off a few inches past.

Ron squinted at it. 'Sure, but ... so what is that?'

'You tell me and we'll both know. You can see where it was rubbing against the rotor.' Dean realised he was holding the crumpled pedal and crank from a bicycle. A small bicycle. 'Last night, that boy, the one missing for ten years? You said he was riding a BMX when he disappeared.'

Ron's face was suddenly as white and damp as a cold glass of milk. 'Holy shit,' he said, drawing out the vowels. 'It must've happened. Holy shit.'

'You said it was a certain colour.'

'I'm not sure I said what colour it was.'

Dean's stomach coiled, his fingertips buzzing against the pedal. 'Blue, Ron. You said that bike was blue.'

***

Reality TV

Paddy O'Reilly

In the make-up room a woman with hair dyed black and glossy as a crow pushed tan foundation into Carly's pores the way you would putty a cracked wall. She had already whipped Carly's hair into a concoction the shape of a soft-top ice-cream. Now she coloured Carly's eyebrows mahogany and her eyelids wine-grape purple.

'The studio lights bleach colours,' she said. 'If I don't do this you'll look like a ghost.'

Carly closed her eyes as a tissue was pasted to her face. When the make-up woman peeled away the tissue, the imprint of a colourful clown mask came away with it.

'All done. Enjoy the show.'

She unclipped the napkin from Carly's neck and stood back, waiting with her hands on her hips while Carly gathered her handbag and coat and tried to get up out of the chair without seeing her gaudy make-up again in the mirror.

Next room down the hall was the Green Room.

It is exactly where she knows it will be. A table beside the door is loaded with plates of half-eaten crusty old sandwiches and limp slivers of cantaloupe and honeydew melon. A grey-haired man sits in the far corner of the room tapping on a laptop. He is probably an actor or director Virginia worked with at the Queens Theatre.

'Hi,' Carly says, not too loudly, but loudly enough for an older man to hear.

He looks up.

'I was just going to introduce myself. I'm Virginia's sister. We might have met?'

'Virginia?' His fingers are still tracing along the trackpad as though his brain has gone on working out a problem while he gazes blankly at Carly. He could be a fixture of the room, an automaton. He'll be working at that computer into eternity as other guests come and go, as programs rise and fall in the ratings, as television itself disappears into electronic obscurity.

'Virginia Sherman. Who the show's about today.'

'No, I don't know her.' He folds back over his laptop.

The door swings open, knocking Carly further into the room.

'Jesus, sorry! Are you all right?' A young man presses his hands gently on different parts of her body as if he is checking for broken bones.

Without warning Carly wants to cry.

This is what she expected to happen. She would walk into a television studio and tell a funny story about her talented movie star sister to a crowd of adoring fans. Next week this scene would be broadcast to a national audience in the millions. Carly's painted face and her cone of hair would be splashed across the nation while Carly relived the nightmare on the couch in her lounge room as the hard drive recorded her for posterity. She'd push aside the comforting arms of her husband and cry in jags and sob about having been born the dumpy, awkward sister, the failure, the plain one. This is what would happen when she stepped onto the stage of *This Is Your Life*. Her resentment, her jealousy, barely concealed, rolling across the screen for the entertainment of friends, enemies and strangers. What could be worse?

'Yes, I'm fine,' she told the young man, slipping back into her usual acquiescent self. 'Let's get this over with.'

'I'll take you to the side of the stage. You'll be able to hear yourself being introduced. Step onto the white marker tape at the edge of the stage and wait till your eyes adjust to the stage lights. Then you'll hear Mac ask you to come on stage. Someone will escort you to your seat.' He was saying all this as they wound their way through dark corridors that smelled like old cheese.

'I'll never find my way back,' she joked, but it wasn't a joke. She thought of poor lost Persephone. When she taught the Year Tens the Persephone story, they told her it was no big deal to live half the year in hell. 'We already do, Missus,' Ari said. 'It's called school.'

The kind young man smiled. 'That's all right. I'll come and get you when you're done.' His hand touched Carly's elbow to prompt her each time they had to turn a corner. He had a downy blonde fuzz where he was probably trying to grow a beard, and his pants were too short. An innocent child was guiding her into this dirty entertainment world.

They pass through a section of the corridor where the lights have failed. The sudden darkness leaches sight from her eyes.

Carly grasps the sleeve of the young man. He whispers to her to be brave, that if she can stay strong it will be over before she knows it. Endurance, that's all she needs – to endure until things reach their natural end. Carly isn't sure exactly what he's talking about.

They come into light again and she laughs with a sick feeling in her belly and she almost wants to turn back into the darkness.

'Endure,' he whispers again, pushing her in the small of the back with more force than she expected, propelling her forward.

They reach the maw of the stage. The boy nudges her forward a further few centimetres. 'Hang on till you hear yourself invited onstage. I'll be waiting back here when it's over.' He turns and sprints away down the dark passage, leaving her at the threshold.

When Carly told the other teachers about the show they interrogated her. 'Are you going to meet anyone famous besides your sister?' 'When will it be broadcast?' 'What will you wear?' They sent out sparks of thrill and anxiety and envy as if this was the most important thing that would ever happen to Carly, as if she was getting what everyone else wanted without having earned it. 'But you hardly ever watch TV!' one complained.

From the shadows at the side of the stage, the lights were so bright Carly couldn't see who was on the stage. There was only an eye-stinging brilliance and the sound of many hands applauding. She stepped onto the white tape that marked the boundary between this world and the next. Her eyes closed involuntarily against the glare.

The boy had said Mac would introduce her. Who was Mac? The usual host was Roger Young. He would stand to the side at the beginning of the show, holding the big red book and reading out facts about the person's life so you could try to guess who it might be before the curtains swept open and the chosen person was revealed.

'And what did she say about this?' Carly heard a man say in a rich caramel voice.

'She doesn't know,' Virginia answered.

'Well then,' the man who must be Mac said, 'perhaps it's time she found out.'

     PADDY O'REILLY

For a stupid moment Carly wondered if the episode was about her and her life. A pathetic flame of ambition flared in her and died. As if she'd had any kind of life worth talking about.

Her eyes are adjusting to the glare. An audience of women on raked seats faces the stage. A man sits high on the steps in the aisle between banks of audience members. He is holding a microphone and speaking towards the stage. He has a head of hair a woman would envy, thick, curly and golden. The hair of a god, or a luscious incubus. His face is familiar, soft-focus familiar, in the way photos of movie stars are familiar, or the story that you start to tell someone and for a blinding moment of confusion you wonder if it was a dream or a sitcom plot or if it actually happened.

All she needed to do was give the speech and sit down and smile. Perhaps kiss Virginia on the cheek and hug her the way she used to when they met in public.

The stage was nothing more than the floor in front of the audience. Virginia, Carly's glamorous actress sister, sat in a chair beside Carly's husband, cradling his hand on her lap. Cradling his hand in her lap and gazing into his face.

For a moment Carly's body is caught in a strange willy willy. Her scalp stings as if her hair is being torn from her head. She retches. Something is scratching at her ankles – claws or thorns or unkempt fingernails. Then the willy willy passes, leaving her uncannily calm.

Mac lounged on the steps between two banks of raked audience seats. He invited Carly to come in as if they were in his living room. Like a starstruck teenager she stepped into the light. A slant to the floor caused her to lurch and totter towards Glenn and Virginia. Her husband and her sister. She repeated it in her head. Husband and sister. Fucking.

Glenn couldn't or wouldn't look in her direction. She had only seen him three hours ago, at breakfast this morning, where he was his usual surly morning self, grunting at the coffee maker and pulling on his suit jacket while he chewed at a piece of toast.

How could he be here?

'Ladies and gentlemen, Mrs Carly Kantzakis,' Mac said, his voice rebounding from the studio's make-believe walls. 'Someone help the lady.'

Amid a cacophony of whistles and shouts and jeers from the audience, a man in a tight t-shirt bounced over to her and gripped her upper arm with his massive hand.

'This way, lady,' he muttered. He half-lifted Carly to the podium where an empty chair faced her sister and her husband.

She feels surprisingly flat. Perhaps it is shock. Perhaps you lose your sense of humiliation and rage under stage lights. She doesn't feel much at all, and that seems wrong. She crosses her legs, hears the rasp of stocking on stocking. Does it again the other way, hears it again. Time stops once more, a space of silence and stillness as she crosses and recrosses her legs in a queer seated dance. After a period that is nothing but the movement of her legs in their rhythmic nonsense scissoring, the sound comes back, distant at first, a crowd from afar, growing louder until she lifts her face and rage smashes up against her calm.

Mac leaned in. 'Carly, I think you've guessed what's going on here. How do you feel?'

The camera rolled towards her. She wished she could wipe off the lurid painted face but it was too late for that. It was too late, wasn't it?

Mac cleared his throat to get the attention of the crowd before he lifted the microphone to his lips.

'Carly, do you have anything to say to your sister? Your husband?'

She raised her head. Why would they do this? Was Virginia broke again? Stupid alcoholic Glenn had no idea what he was getting into. Carly had lived with Princess Virginia and her neediness all her life.

The calls from the studio audience were gathering like a rehearsed chorus into a chant and accompanying clap.

'Car–ly. Car–ly. Car–ly.'

It makes her smile. As if she is the famous sister, the one loved by the tabloids. Is this how it feels to be golden? People calling to her. Her name turned into a song. Mac smiles at her as if he is privy to every thought in her mind. She turns her face away, blushing. When she glances back he is still smiling at her. Space and time are curving around her body, tucking her into a tight uncomfortable fold as Mac reads her mind and keeps smiling that knowing smile.

From the corner of her eye Carly could see the iris of the camera widen to take in the whole scene. She knew the kind

     PADDY O'REILLY

of thing they were hoping she'd say, the weeping and shrieking they wanted her to do. She grew up with television and its conventions. She had laughed at the women on shows like this who lunged at their betraying husbands, tried to hit them with weak half-closed fists, who moaned and wept, who bared themselves.

Carly didn't want to be one of those women. She was here on stage, betrayed, sure enough, but by a man she had already grown to despise. Sitting in the blindingly bright studio watched by a crowd of screamers, she could only come up with one thought. The words popped out of her mouth, harmless missiles out of a peashooter. 'Why didn't I leave you years ago?'

A small man holding up a large placard raced backwards and forwards across the studio floor in front of the audience. The placard said *Laugh*. Scattered on the floor at the side of the stage were more that said *Scream* and *Howl* and *Hiss* and other instructions for whatever he wanted the audience to do. Right now they were doing it all at once. A woman in clingy aqua pants barrelled down the stairs, arms flailing, calling out that Carly should punch the dirty bastard. She was caught at the bottom of the steps by two hefty men and escorted backstage to the cheering of the crowd.

Mac stood. He tamped down the noise with hand gestures until there were only a few catcalls coming from the back rows.

'Glenn? Would I be wrong in saying your wife doesn't seem as surprised as you expected?'

Glenn's upper lip curled in that special way Carly used to find sexy. 'Don't believe that shit. She's surprised all right. This is her fake *I don't give a damn* routine. The one I've put up with for nine years.'

'Hey!' an angry voice shouted down from one of the back rows of the crowd. A slim woman in jeans and t-shirt with her hair in two girlish pigtails sprang out of her seat. 'You didn't like your wife? Why'd you stay? Why didn't you run off with the famous sister instead of humiliating this woman here on TV?'

As the crowd applauded, Glenn looked off to the side. He sighed, the way he did with Carly when he had no answer to a question and he wanted to pretend the question was stupid to begin with. But the woman wasn't taking any of that. She pushed aside the blonde next to her and clambered across three more people to reach the aisle. A stagehand raced up the stairs to hold a microphone in front of her face.

'You answer me, mate. Why are you doing this?'

Virginia lifted the stage microphone and murmured into it. 'It's not his fault. We fell in love. We didn't know how to tell her.'

'You shut up, you washed-up hack!'

Virginia shook her head, lip trembling, features emulsified into the vulnerable haunted face that got her into movies in the first place.

Pigtail woman jabbed her scarlet-nailed finger at Virginia. 'A slut like you took my husband away too but at least she didn't go on national television to tell me.'

Carly starts when she hears that line, 'A slut like you took my husband away but at least she didn't go on national television to tell me.' The line is thrumming through her. She's heard it before, but where?

'Steady, ladies,' Mac interrupted. He'd been moving around the studio, stopping at the bottom of the rows of seats before strolling across to the side of the stage where Carly, Virginia and Glenn sat. Now he came to rest behind Carly, where he placed an icy hand on her shoulder as he spoke over her head to Virginia. 'Virginia, what do you need to say to Carly?'

'No, stop.' Carly surged out of her seat. 'I'm not going on with this. I won't give permission for it to be broadcast.' She'd received the contract in the mail, seen her sister's name as the feature of the show, glanced at the clauses on the first page about network serial repeat rights and other TV jargon, and signed without reading any further.

Placard man scooted up and down in front of the audience rows again. The shiny eager faces responded with boos and hisses and foot stamping.

'Forget it.' Carly turned to the rows of angry faces. 'I'm not going to be your freak show. Find someone else.'

Behind her, Mac spoke to the audience in a conspiratorial whisper. 'Ladies, don't you find it amazing that no one, absolutely no one, reads the fine print of contracts. I would have thought our Carly here, a teacher of all things, would have read what she was getting herself into.'

'So sue me.' There was nothing to stop her leaving.

Or so she thinks, but when she wheels around and strides to

          PADDY O'REILLY

*the stage entrance she finds two t-shirted brutes standing with
their arms crossed in front of the doorway.*

'Get out of the way.'

*They remain motionless. Carly pushes her arm between them
and tries to shove her shoulder through, the way you would at
a gate that won't open properly. The men don't budge. They're
welded together like the two-headed dog at the gates of hell.*

The crowd was screaming, laughing, hooting. Rage percolated
in Carly's gut. She muttered threats at the guardians about
lawsuits, keeping her voice down and her back to the cameras.
She found herself hissing at them like a cat. 'I will not let this
happen. I will not accept this.'

'My, my.' Mac had climbed the audience steps again and was
looking down. 'Carly seems to have found her inner fury. So
Glenn, I guess this isn't the ice queen you were telling us about.'

'Stop filming me!' Carly shouted, still facing away from the
crowd and the cameras and Mac. 'I refuse to allow this.'

She certainly couldn't look at Virginia and Glenn. Glenn, who
had been telling this mad chorus that she was an ice queen.
Glenn who chewed nicotine gum sixteen hours a day. Glenn who
had a swatch of wiry ginger hair at the base of his spine that she
could no longer bear to touch. Glenn who had lusted after her
sister from the moment he saw her. Her sister – spendthrift,
actress, star, family favourite. Selfish witch. They deserved
each other but Carly could not look at them because she was on
TV. Everyone would see every move she made. She was on her
way to becoming an ugly reality star, and she'd watched enough
TV and read enough magazines to know what that meant.

She would not give Virginia and Glenn the satisfaction. She
would not give them the airtime, the gloating, the happiness
they thought this alliance might provide them. Shame had
filled her, shame and rage and a new iron stubbornness. She
would not endure this humiliation.

The cameras on their dollies wheeled around the studio floor
trying to capture her face in all its grim shame while she sidled
to a corner and faced the wall like a naughty child at school.

'I have to say, ladies, this is not great television.' Mac sighed.
'What can we do to bring Carly out of her shell? Hmm?'

The chant started up again.

'Car–ly. Car–ly. Car–ly.'

'Tell those bastards what you think, Carly! We're on your side,' one woman screamed.

No one was on Carly's side. That, at least, was clear.

'Go on, Carly!'

'Smack that bitch, Carly!'

'Car–ly. Car–ly. Car–ly. Car–ly. Car–ly.'

They think they can unleash her rage. They are wrong. How strange her name sounds when it becomes a chant from the audience. It could be someone else's name. Car – ly. Ka – li, she realises. Kali. Religions of the world, Year Eight. Kali, the goddess of destruction and change. Can you destroy by doing nothing? Can you banish by not accepting?

She remained perfectly still in her corner, refusing to turn around. As long as she didn't participate there was no show.

The shouting from the crowd slowly died down. The audience members began to chat amongst themselves. Mac raced down the stairs and murmured over her shoulder, promised her a chance to respond with dignity. He held out a hand as if something she might want rested in the palm. The hand was empty.

She ignored him and waited. The warm-up comedian faced down the mutinous audience, cajoled a few laughs, ran out of material. Mac, leaning over her shoulder and speaking so close to her face that his breath heated her cheek, threatened her with lawsuits. She waited.

The show's producer hurried onto the stage. He rode the other shoulder, his muttering a spray of warm spit. Time passed and her legs ached with tension and she needed to go to the toilet but she closed her eyes, her ears, her mind, and waited.

The stage manager ordered the operators to shut down the cameras. The big lights went off with a clank. She waited.

People chattered as they edged across the rows. She heard the rumble and clatter as they filed down the staircase and out through the exit. One or two called out to her. 'Goodbye, Carly!' 'Good luck, Carly. Stick it to him!'

After long moments in the dark of the shut-down stage, she felt someone behind her. A warm presence, a scent of pine. A hand touched her arm. Her body had tipped forward with the rigidity of a board leaning against the wall. Her forehead pressed against the flimsy studio partition. She stared at her feet, knotted that morning, an aeon ago, a minute ago, into the

     PADDY O'REILLY

straps of her best silver high heels. She remembered that time she woke from a dream where actors from her favourite TV drama were carrying her in an open coffin.

'You can turn around now.' The young man who had led her to this place stood with his hand out to take hers. 'They've shut down the cameras. The audience is gone.'

'Is it over?' she asked.

'I'm afraid not,' he said. 'Let's go.'

Everything had fizzled and left an eerie dim silence, an electric loneliness, like the empty drawn-out moment when the TV is turned off.

She takes hold of his forearm and follows him out to the corridor, weak and prickly with the leftover adrenalin of her emotional storm. All she wants to do is go home, lie down, take a few days off work. It has been hellish – unbelievable, really – but she stood her ground. She would not talk this through with those betrayers, not on reality TV, not in her home, not anywhere. Never.

All she wants to do is sleep. So tired she is dizzy. Things have taken on a dreamy quality. Is she asleep, dreaming? There is tiredness, yes, but there's more. A kind of echo of time passing, or moving. A swirling, eddying sense of the movement of time.

Back in the make-up room, the woman was waiting for Carly. She held a sponge already loaded with tan foundation. Carly sat down in the chair. The make-up woman looked familiar. She was probably one of the parents Carly had talked with at some parent–teacher day.

The woman stroked the first bars of tan colour onto Carly's white skin.

'The studio lights are hell,' she said. 'They bleach out colours. If I don't do this—'

***

Truth and Reconciliation

Ali Alizadeh

The frames of the opening credits for this week's *Words from the Heart* have been accelerated. The accompanying soundtrack has a new urgency. It seems the tune has been rerecorded at a faster tempo, and its rhythm has been replaced with a pressing digital drum beat.

This subtly different version of the show's opening has its intended effect on the millions of people watching the popular program not only across the United States but in every part of our Global Village. They, and those joining Diva Aphrodite's audience for the first time this evening due to the sensational subject of her live interview, are galvanised by the hurried succession of images – beaming faces of countless celebrities who have spoken to Diva about their lives and loves and suchlike over the years – on flat screen TVs, computer monitors, laptops and smart phones.

It's not only the monumentally important content of tonight's show – an immeasurably famous yet mysterious guest who has been in the news for the last two months, accused of a most unspeakable crime, finally breaking his silence to the *Empress of American Television* – but also the skilfully intensified aesthetics of the program which have entranced many millions of viewers. There is no doubt in anyone's mind that they are about to witness nothing less than history in the making.

Diva's warm, wise, botoxed and foundationed face invades the screens. 'Welcome, friends, to another episode of *Words from the Heart*. Before I introduce you to tonight's guest, let me thank everyone who has written in to express their support for last week's guest, the actor Chucky Spleen. His tale of courage and survival and triumphant return to the silver screen has touched many hearts, and I must say, it is interviews like that and responses like yours that make this job worthwhile. Now—'

Hers is a kindly if somewhat overly beautified face, an effect which, of course, should not be misinterpreted as her make-up team's ineptitude. This look is a carefully calculated strategy to make Diva, America's richest living (or dead) woman, appear like an Everywoman, understandably anxious about her

　　　　ALI ALIZADEH

blemishes and wrinkles. Her face, at any rate, turns rather cold. 'Well, tonight I'd like to tell you a different story. Or perhaps let you hear it from the man at the centre of one of the most notorious, controversial and talked-about events of our time.

'We have all heard the allegations about doping, about the bribing of officials and about what has been described as the greatest sporting scandal in history. I am of course referring to the case surrounding Jack Knuckletov, the ten-time winner of the world's most important crawl-hopping event, Tour de Normandy.

'Jack is an American legend, an inspiration to millions of young crawl-hoppers around the world, and the founder of eight charity organisations, six orphanages in sub-Saharan Africa, and the owner of the world's largest distillery specialising in producing organic, low-carb, non-alcoholic aperitifs.

'But are the allegations true? Has one of our greatest national icons, the man described by the Nobel Peace Prize Laureate Okumala Quacka as an inspiration to millions of poor crawl-hopping children around the world, has this man – estimated to be worth \$500 billion in corporate sponsorship and religious donations – been taking banned performance enhancing drugs and lying to his hundreds of millions of fans for more than a decade?'

Diva's face has remained more or less expressionless through-out the heart-stopping introduction. But her eyes have widened ever so slightly to convey a simmering sense of excitement fused with a hint of indignation.

She takes a deep, meaningful breath as the camera pans out to show, positioned opposite Diva on an exquisite armchair, the gaunt figure and bony face of one of the world's most recognisable athletes – that is, one of the planet's most exulted living beings – appearing visibly uneasy (the assiduous make-up team have sprayed droplets of quality fake perspiration to the legendary persona's forehead to accentuate the outward expression of his inner moral turmoil).

'Welcome to *Words from the Heart*, Jack.'

'It's so good to be on your show, Diva.'

Diva grants Knuckletov the same ambiguous smile that she perfected for her interview with the human rights activist and alleged child molester Melinda Bates.

'More from me and the world crawl-hopping champion Jack Knuckletov, in his first and only media interview in recent months, right after this break.'

The viewers are annoyed by the interruption but, needless to say, they're far too expectant to lose interest or turn off their screens. Australian spectators cast their eyes on a dazzling Outback desert, to the soundtrack of an '80s stadium rock ballad. It's an advertisement for a car, a 4WD that bounces effortlessly on the vivid sand dunes. It costs only $85,000. Then a sagacious ex-football hero, with distinguished white hair and fake professorial glasses, announces the benefits of applying for a new credit card from *the nation's most reliable bank*. Buckets of popcorn and ice-cream are ravaged as the final commercial for this break promises a secluded tropical beach manned – womanned, actually – by a solitary semi-naked being strolling lazily in the shade of dreamy palm trees.

Diva smiles fleetingly before resuming her hardest interrogator's facial expression. 'Welcome back to the show. I'm speaking to Jack Knuckletov, in his first and only media interview in recent months.'

Cut to Knuckletov's face. There's fear, or hunger, in his narrow eyes.

'Jack. Let me be direct and ask you what all Americans and all people of the world have been waiting to hear from your own lips.'

Knuckletov is the picture of strained politeness.

'Sure, Diva.'

'Did you at any point during your career as the Captain of the United States of America's Crawl-Hopping Team take performance enhancing drugs?'

Knuckletov breathes heavily (and the depth and weight of his seminal breaths are captured and enhanced by a microphone strategically interred in the folds of his collar).

'Jack?'

'Yes. I did, Diva.'

'Did you at any point take any banned substances that strengthened the muscles of your buttocks and anus, giving you an unfair advantage in the sport of crawl-hopping?'

'Yes, Diva.'

Diva's voice grows in volume and alacrity.

     ALI ALIZADEH

'Did you take steroids, BMPs, ST5s, T98Fs, and prohibited quantities of Viagra?'

'Yes. I did.'

'Did you bribe Tour de Normandy officials to replace your urine, spool, sperm, skin, toenail and pubic hair samples with uncontaminated samples?'

Jack pauses to have a noisy sip of water from a glittering crystal cup.

'Jack?'

'Yes, Diva. I did that.'

'Did you compel or encourage the other members of the United States of America's Crawl-Hopping Team to take banned performance enhancing drugs?'

Jack's voice is becoming almost inaudible.

'Yes, Diva. That is correct.'

Diva's excited face conquers the screen. She is now flagrantly beaming. 'More from me and the world crawl-hopping champion Jack Knuckletov right after this.'

People are stunned and filled with horror and joy. Even though the overwhelming majority have lives permanently bedevilled by debt, exploitation and unfulfilled needs, what they have just witnessed has profoundly distracted them from their miseries. Could this be the most engrossing thing on TV since the 9/11 terror attacks? Meanwhile, a very sexy, vivacious young woman – who claims to be a caring mother, the CEO of a company and a loving wife – talks about the radical new environmentally-friendly lotion that helps her skin look young and helps her stay regular at the same time. Then a middle-aged couple extol the benefits of early cancer detection technology. Finally, a radical new line of anti-depressants inaugurates the dawn of a bright new era of confidence, love and happiness.

Diva untightens her lips.

'Welcome back to the show. Jack, I bet everyone at home is dying to ask you this. Why? Why did you do it?'

Knuckletov has most probably had a shot of whisky during the break. He has regained his voice. 'Can I first say that I'm really happy to be able to tell my side of the story, Diva. I'm so glad that you've given me the chance to finally come clean. Thank you, Diva. And I wanna thank your audience too.'

Diva grins knowingly.

'Could you please answer the question, Jack? You were the champion crawl-hopper at Harvard. You were the most talented young crawl-hopper of your generation. Why did you cheat?'

'Yes, Diva. I did cheat. I cheated and lied to myself, to my family, and to my fans. For many years. And for that I am very, very, very sorry. If only I could go back in time and compete in the sport fairly. But, you know, Diva—'

'Yes, Jack?'

'When you're out there, in front of huge crowds, representing your country and your sport, you feel so pressured, so keen to impress everyone, and if you're as young and naive as I was, you can't help but be tempted to do what everyone else is doing. I mean, you know, there's a lot of doping going on in elite sport.'

Diva seems unimpressed.

'Even if that were the case, Jack, even if all of that were true, I don't see why you've been denying the allegations made by your former teammates for the past five months. You've even sued some of them for defamation.'

Knuckletov closes his eyes. He opens them after five seconds of the lens of the studio camera inching towards his moistening eye sockets.

'Like I said, Diva. I'm really, really sorry.'

Diva is almost conspicuously irate, or perhaps intensely bemused.

'When did it start, Jack?'

Knuckletov dries his eyes and asks for more water.

'At the 2002 Tour. I was only 23 then. I had been training for more than three years to qualify to join the United States team. And, you know Diva, I knew I wasn't fast enough to win. The Chinese and the Africans were so much faster than any American crawl-hopper. They had stronger knees, tighter arse cheeks, stronger hands. And, like, everyone knew that they were doping. And I guess we should've just gone to the authorities and reported them, but everyone knew the people running the Tour were corrupt, so, you know, if you can't beat them, you might as well join them.'

'I'm not sure I'd agree with that logic, Jack.'

Knuckletov is now smiling dreamily.

'No American had ever won a Tour before me, Diva. And

　ALI ALIZADEH

I thought, what the hey! Why not! And when I climbed the podium after hopping over the finish line ahead of the Chinese and Russians and Africans and Indians and everyone else, it was really, really amazing. To stand there and to feel that I had made the people of this country proud of me. It was ... an incredible feeling.'

Diva seems reflective. She nods and turns to the camera.

'More after this.'

Boxes of tissue are passed around. And then the preview of the new Chucky Spleen movie, *Snakeman 5*. A 3D tour de force featuring much fighting, skyscrapers being climbed, nubile co-star being seduced, and earnest lines – e.g. 'It's a hell of a thing, being a good guy in a place like this ...' – prior to a sneak peek of the frank new reality TV drama, *Border Control Girls*, in which five female coastguard officers explore asylum seeker policy and intimate sexual matters – e.g. 'We were like on our way to intercept a refugee boat when I got the call from Steve, you know, the guy from the surf club, saying he wanted to see me again, and I thought, oh my god ...' – followed by a pre-recorded announcement by Diva Aphrodite to the members of her official fan club. 'Friends, will you help me in putting an end to domestic violence? Call this number or visit our website to donate to a truly worthwhile cause.'

Diva returns in real time.

'Welcome back everyone. I'm talking to Jack Knuckletov about the pressures of being an elite athlete. Jack, tell me about some of the non-profit organisations you've founded over the years.'

'Sure, Diva. You know, what I'm most proud of is the Live Tough Foundation. It's for underprivileged Native American kids who've survived testicular cancer and have ADHD. Can we show—'

'Oh yes. Here, we have some footage of Jack and some of the kids he has helped.'

Saccharine music, and two minutes of slow-motion hugs between the famous crawl-hopper and excessively happy, overweight teenagers.

'Really inspiring stuff, Jack. Reminds me of last week's guest Chucky Spleen's work for SESF, Save the Endangered Stingrays Foundation.'

'Oh, yeah, I'm a huge fan of that one. Stingrays are such beautiful creatures.'

'Aren't they?'

'And the Chinese hunt them with such cruelty, it just breaks my heart.'

Diva appears to be in agreement.

'Speaking of sad things, Jack, is it true that you and your wife, world cross-skimming champion Stella Rhododendron are getting a divorce? Is this something you feel comfortable to talk to me about?'

'Well, you know, Diva, all the media scrutiny over the last few months, all the accusations, have been really hurtful, and, as you know, Stella is no stranger to any of that, but still, it's been pretty tough on us all, and, you know, I just wanna get on with my life with the Live Tough Foundation and save more Native American lives.'

'So are you separating? There's been a lot of speculation.'

'Look, Stella and me have always been there for each other, and we've been through a lot together. So, let's just say we're not about to make any rushed decisions. She's the love of my life, you know. She's a really amazing woman, so kind, and she's donated so much money to so many charities.'

'She certainly is an incredible person. We received lots of letters and emails after having her on the show last year. I'm so glad to see that unfortunate incident with her being accused of ruining the career of former world cross-skimming champion Bella Rosenbloom is all behind her.'

'That's right, Diva. All those baseless accusations of Stella paying someone to hack into Bella's computer, and then sending photos of Bella having sex with five married men to the media, all of that was just really cruel and hurtful. Like, you know, the accusations that people have been making against me.'

Diva raises her eyebrows.

'But, Jack, you've just admitted to doping.'

'Yes, I know, Diva, but like I said, that's all behind me now, and I just wanna get on with saving disadvantaged kids, adopting more children from Ghana and Yemen, helping empower the women of Mozambique and Pakistan, saving the pristine tundras of Alaska and, you know, I've just decided to set up a new program to sponsor research into reducing greenhouse

     ALI ALIZADEH

gas emissions of social networking websites for people with disabilities.'

Diva lowers her eyebrows and nods.

'Sounds wonderful. More after this break.'

Beyond the eyes and minds entrenched in *Words from the Heart*, outside of living rooms and office cubicles and spectral zones where faces are fixated on magnetic screens, something like reality wrestles with ideology, and fails. The viewers feel docile and relieved to live in a world where truth and reconciliation are enabled by a soulful media personality. For the coveted final ad break two opposing campaign messages announce the intentions of the leaders of the two major political parties competing for office in the upcoming federal election. Both feature Australian flags, graciously smiling mothers and overjoyed children, flourishing farms and a burgeoning ecosystem. The thinner party leader promises to protect Australia's borders against illegal refugees, fight global warming, protect Australian jobs from foreign competition, cut tax and help small business. The fatter party leader promises to resolve the asylum seeker issue, fight global warming, help working families in these harsh financial times, bring down the cost of living and help small business. Then there's a commercial for waterproof nappies.

'Welcome back everyone to the final part of my conversation with Jack Knuckletov. As we've been saying, the world needs more people who are prepared to make sacrifices to make things better for everyone. Jack, who is your inspiration?'

'My father, Diva. He was a poor immigrant from the former Soviet Union. He decided that he didn't want to live and have a family in a totalitarian state. So he migrated to America so that his children would be born in a free, democratic country.'

'Is he still alive?'

'Oh yeah, and he's been very supportive of me and Stella over the past few months.'

'There's nothing like family, is there, Jack?'

'You're absolutely right, Diva. He's been just incredible. You know, he didn't speak a word of English when he moved to this country. He owned nothing but the clothes on his back.'

'What about your mother, Jack? Where was she from?'

'Oh she was a … dancer, from New Jersey. She met my dad after a show. It was love at first sight.'

Diva suppresses a yawn.

'Well, it's been a pleasure having you on the show, Jack. I must say, I was a little concerned at first about how things would go, but it's been lovely to talk to you.'

'Thank you, Diva.'

Diva Aphrodite addresses the camera for the last time this evening.

'Now, in next week's show we'll meet an inspiring woman who three years ago decided to take control of her own life. You might not know of her yet, but you'll be hearing a lot more about her soon. An incredible true story of courage, success, and the American dream. Until then, *ciao* everyone.'

The end credits are slow and lacklustre. We have time to empty our bowels and bladders before the next show. Jack Knuckletov and Diva Aphrodite should be given the Nobel Peace Prize. Who'll be the next Australian Prime Minster? Oh, well. Slums of Third World megacities will expand as shall the waistlines of First World's fast food addicted underclass. Bread riots and erotic fan fiction shall compete for news headlines. What's on next? Repeats of *The Twilight Zone*?! I'm not sure if we're up for it. A bit too weird and creepy for our liking.

***

　　　　　ALI ALIZADEH

A Void

Guy Salvidge

Awake, my dreams already fading. Awake to warmth, to dimness, to a tumble of blankets and sheets. Someone else in the bed, softly murmuring. I rub my eyes and peer. A slim, naked back, a tangle of dark hair on the other pillow. The room is dark, the blinds shutting out the incipient day, but my eyes are adjusting. Dust motes hang in a narrow shard of sunlight. The bed is warm but the world is cold; a big toe poking out from the bottom of the sheet informs me of this. It is all the exploration I wish to do today.

She turns toward me, eyes slitted. A face without a name.

'Tyler Bramble,' she says, teasing me. 'You've forgotten my name, haven't you? Poor sap.'

I reach out to her and she presses my hand to her breast. Her skin is hot, her core a furnace. 'You seem familiar, but yes,' I admit. 'It'll come to me in a minute.'

'I'll save us both the suspense; I'm Lily Follicle.' She smiles and I am drawn towards her by some bodily convection. I stir and press myself against her. 'My, you're keen,' she says. 'I'd have thought I'd worn you out last night.'

Of this I remember nothing. 'So how was I?'

She shrugs. 'So-so.'

'That's all I get? So-so?'

'I was tossing up between that and meh.'

She throws off the covers and rises into the frigidity, leaving me clinging to the corner of the blanket. She is slender and petite, and mustn't feel the cold for she slinks off into the bathroom naked, her breath visible, and shuts the door behind her. After a few seconds I hear the shower.

The commbox, my electronic ball and chain, is winking red on the sideboard, displaying urgent, unread messages. Then, for me, it is a scramble for clothes without thought of 'clean' or 'dirty'. I dress in what comes to hand, groping around the edges of the bed. I pull on layer after layer until the cold is vanquished. Soon I am myself again, not a cowering, craven, bed-ridden weakling but a man of stature, of import. A Seeker, though admittedly an unwashed one.

Only then do I consider the commbox, just as the shower ceases.

Two messages, both from Garrick, my superior.

The first reads:

Meet me at the French fountain at Carlton Gardens. Something's up.

The message is time-stamped 07:55. The current time on the commbox reads 08:57.

The second message, sent just fifteen minutes ago, says:

I need you down here in a hurry, Tyler.

The bathroom door opens and Lily emerges in a cloud of steam. She's wrapped in one of my towels. 'No more playtime?' she asks.

'I've got to go,' I say. 'Perhaps later this evening?' I can see heat rising from her naked shoulders.

'You'll be lucky.' She goes over to the window, spreads the blinds. We peer down at the frozen city. Nothing much moves at street level. 'You don't want to go out there, not today,' she says. Then she pads over to the bed and starts looking for her clothes. I go into the bathroom and do what I need to do there. When I come out, she's dressed in standard office attire: red blouse, black skirt, low heels. No jacket, nothing warm at all.

'You off to work, too?' I ask her.

She nods. 'I work for Professor Eardrum. I'm his personal assistant.'

The look on her face seems to suggest that I ought to recognise this name. 'I see,' I offer.

She picks up the commbox from the sideboard and hefts it. 'You don't remember him either. Your memory's going.'

I admit that this is so, but I'm impatient to get moving. Garrick rarely leaves Seeker Bureau, and when he does it's invariably with good cause. I envisage him stamping his feet by the French fountain, kicking at the wet leaves in annoyance. I gather my things, my .22 revolver among them. Then I take the commbox back from Lily and shove it in a deep pocket in my trenchcoat.

'You ought to remember the professor,' Lily says. We face one another. She's applied red lipstick. 'You met me at his party last night. He introduced us.'

I realise that I don't have a hangover. My head, for once, is clear. 'Was I drinking?'

     GUY SALVIDGE

'Not drinking, no. You were kind of uptight.'

I nod, having no memory of the previous night. It is as though Eardrum's party never happened, but then I have no other memory to offer as evidence against it. Lily stares at me and I know that she knows I'm trying and failing to remember.

'You could use a shave, Tyler. Maybe something for breakfast. And stay off the booze, for your own sake.'

'I don't normally eat first thing in the morning,' I counter. 'And I'm growing a beard.' I gesture to the door. 'Shall we?'

I shut the door behind us and we descend the stairs to the Ballard's lobby. There's no one at reception, no one behind the desk. This is not in itself unusual, but it unnerves me all the same.

'You'll catch your death of cold dressed like that,' I tell Lily as we step out onto the street. A stiff, freezing wind batters us. I should have put on my gloves. I ought to offer Lily the use of my trenchcoat, but I don't.

But Lily is unperturbed. She grins. 'I have a very fast metabolism. See you at Eardrum's.'

And before I can ask her any of the pertinent questions that this second statement raises – when? where? why? – she disappears into a nearby alley. I hasten after her, but she's vanished. I look for her, but not for long. She'll find me again if she wants to.

So.

There's ice on the pavement, but now that the sun is up it's starting to melt into puddles. It's a weekday and yet the normal hubbub of inner-city Melbourne is notably – and perplexingly – absent. Power outage, perhaps? The trams are running as usual. The city is not entirely devoid of humanity, but I estimate that where one hundred people might normally bustle, today there bustles ten. Could it be a public holiday that I've forgotten about? As Garrick noted, something's up.

On Bourke Street, I step onto the 96 tram and stand near the rear door, ignoring the many vacant seats. The traffic is exceptionally light for this time of day. The tram sails through major intersections unimpeded and turns onto Nicholson. The commuters on the tram behave as I'd expect them to, ignoring one another. There's a heater above me but it barely seems to take away the chill. I rub my hands together.

'They say it's a cold snap,' a fortyish woman – about my age – informs me. She's rugged up in a blood orange parka.

'Who say that?' I ask her.

'They do,' she says, without specifying who. Something is wrong and getting wronger. It's hard to quantify. Despite the cold, it's very bright. I rub the stubble on my face with the palm of my hand, closing my eyes.

> *—Garrick's bulk looms above me, pinning me down. His chest is heaving. His mouth moves, but I hear no sound. My limbs flail but he's got me trapped. Now he raises the knife—*

The woman in the parka is gone. The tram slows to its halt at the museum and I step off. The gardens are all but empty, perhaps not surprising given the bitter cold, and the air swirls with fallen leaves whipped up from the ground. A million more leaves, brown and dead, have blanketed the grass. Cold snap, indeed. The branches of the deciduous trees stand bleak and grey against the harsh, empty sky. I see no clouds and no sun.

Garrick is at the French fountain just the way I had imagined him, stamping his feet and tapping his watch at me, his jowly face ruddy with cold. 'What took you?' he says. 'You're looking old.'

'I'm the oldest I've ever been and, if you must know, I had a visitor spend the night.'

Garrick frowns. 'Something's messing with me and I don't know what it is. Shall we grab a coffee? Then we can get to sleuthing.'

'What's up with your office? Is your heater broken?'

He shakes his head. 'Something's wrong, like I said. Very wrong, perhaps.'

> *—and plunges it into my shoulder, which explodes with fiery pain. I kick out at him and he crumples sideways. The knife is embedded in my flesh—*

I look up at the stone cherubs, their expression serene, their arms interlocked against a backdrop of scintillating spray, and the sky pulses white. A deep groan pours from my mouth and

    GUY SALVIDGE

I stumble forward to the edge of the shallow catchment pool. My foot slips on a thin crust of ice and I tumble into the icy water, smacked doubly by the shock and the concrete. Garrick is above me, reaching out, and in my craze I slap him away and he too slips and falls. Then I am over him, a thunder in my ear, and my hands extend outward but not to assist. My hands go to his throat and commence squeezing. Garrick splutters and chokes, his eyes pleading and his flesh quivering, and I relent. The thunder desists and we drag ourselves up to the leaf-laden bank.

'That's exactly the kind of shit I'm referring to,' Garrick says in a small voice, heaving himself up into a sitting position. He is soaked through and shivering. I am on hands and knees before him. No one has noticed our brief altercation and no one comes to our aid.

'I thought you were trying to kill me,' I say. 'I don't know why.'

'Visions,' he whispers. 'I've been having them myself. I saw you choking me, and then it happened for real. It was a premonition.'

'I saw you stabbing me,' I say. 'I must have panicked.'

'Stabbing you? I don't carry a knife.'

We sit trembling. Neither of us tries to stand. The wind has died down, the flurries of leaves finally at rest. We are so cold that our minds have nearly spluttered out.

'We need to get out of this cold,' I say. 'I can't feel my legs.'

> *—and I wrench it out. I'm facedown in the pool, the water billowing with my blood. A pair of eyes down there at the bottom, looking up. I reach out—*

Garrick and I are back on the tram. I have no memory of how we got here and the expression on his face tells me that neither does he. We are sitting in front of the heater.

'We keep blanking out, both of us,' he says in his normal voice. I can see that he's trying to pull himself together.

'And now we're dry,' I observe. Looking out, I see that we are in East Brunswick, at the start of the 96 tram's route back into the city centre. 'We must have been sat here a while.'

'I hope we remembered to tag on,' Garrick says, indicating to the ticket inspector coming along the aisle. He looks at his watch, but the hands have stopped ticking. 'What time is it?'

I pull out my commbox but it, too, is dead. Perhaps it didn't like being immersed in the fountain.

The ticket inspector asks for our cards and we display them to her satisfaction. 'They've got you in a pocket universe,' she says as she passes us by.

'Excuse me, what did you say?' Garrick asks, but she doesn't turn back and he doesn't press the issue.

We sit without speaking for a while. The museum passes on our right, and then we're back in the CBD.

'I dunno about you, but I'm starting to feel a little better,' Garrick says. 'I could murder a club sandwich.'

The sky is a little less white here, and the visions, though not entirely subdued, are more on the level of nightmarish flights of fancy now. I can banish them from my mind with some effort. 'Why did you want to meet me at the fountain?' I ask.

'Because of something that piece-of-shit professor said. He must've tricked me.'

'Eardrum?'

'Yeah, Eardrum. You know him? Hadn't met the character myself until this morning. Wish I never had.'

'That visitor I mentioned? She's his PA, apparently. A Lily Follicle.'

'Follicle? These are bullshit names, Tyler. Someone's got their claws into us. Come on, I'll buy you a beer. It must be nearly lunch time.'

*

At Young & Jackson's, I bite into my club sandwich and find that I am ravenous for the crispy bacon, the melted cheese, the chunks of chicken breast. The pub is dark and warm. Garrick wolfs his sandwich down in a handful of lusty swallows, then his fingers dive into the bowl of chips between us. I'm not far behind, sauce dribbling down my chin. I wipe my mouth with a napkin and start shovelling chips.

'Since when did you eat like this?' Garrick asks through a mouth filled with half-masticated potato. He swallows and reaches for the bowl. 'Thought you said booze had wrecked your appetite for good.'

'Apparently I was sober last night. Fuck knows why.'

'That Eardrum character, I think I've seen him before. Those two – what did you say his assistant's name was? – they are the common denominator here.' Garrick waves a long chip at me, then bites it in two. He reaches for his pint and takes a long swallow.

'Follicle.'

'What?'

'She's called Lily Follicle.'

'Right, like I was saying.' But he's lost his train of thought.

I take a drink from my own pint and my head feels immediately woozy. I put it down on its coaster, still three-quarters full. It won't go down right today. 'You said you saw Eardrum this morning. What did he want?'

Garrick tilts his head, straining to remember. 'He asked all kinds of questions about my health. How I had slept, any bad dreams.' He's slurring his words. I take the half-finished pint away from him, put it out of his reach. He doesn't seem to notice, instead busying himself with tearing his coaster into pieces.

'And what did you tell him?'

'That as far as I'm concerned, I must have slept like a baby.' He's on the verge of dropping off now, his eyelids fluttering, his body slumping down against the soft, cushiony booth. What remains of the coaster hangs forgotten from his fat fingers.

I grab his hairy wrist, wrench him up. 'Garrick! He's fucked us up, that Eardrum. He's poisoned us.'

'The fucker,' he mutters. 'Another pint?'

'No more drinking,' I say. 'He's drugged us and the alcohol's making it worse.'

'I'm gonna fix him.' His head touches the table-top.

'We'll go straight back to Seeker Bureau, run a profile. Find out where his office is. Garrick?' He's passed out, his huge head on the table next to the empty chip bowl.

'Fuck me,' I say, foraging in my trenchcoat for the commbox. I fish it out. That's right – busted. I consider the two unfinished drinks on the table.

'Bad idea,' a familiar voice says.

I look up and it's Lily Follicle. I shuffle into the corner of the booth and she sits alongside me.

'You're stalking me now?' I ask.

'I'm concerned about the wellbeing of you two, and not without reason,' she replies, gesturing to the prone mass on the other side of the table.

I grab her wrist. 'Take me to Eardrum. I want a word with him.'

She wrenches her hand away, her face flashing with anger. 'That's what I was about to suggest. Don't lose your cool, Tyler. It's about the only endearing quality you have.' She starts rummaging in her handbag.

'What are you doing?'

'He needs a stimulant or there'll be no getting him up for hours.'

'Leave him – you people have done enough.'

She turns to me. 'He'll end up in the drunk tank; won't take long for the bar-staff to take offence. He'll soil himself, I expect.'

Garrick is snoring like a man with a bandsaw tied to his chest.

'Have it your way,' I say.

Lily goes up to the bar and returns promptly with a glass of water, into which she dissolves a sachet of powder. I sidle up to Garrick and try to manhandle him into a sitting position. His hair is oily and damp with sweat. Lily pours some of the concoction into his mouth and he gurgles and rails against her. His eyes snap open. 'What the fuck!' he demands.

'Drink it and you'll feel much better,' Lily says.

To my surprise, he does as instructed, then sits up straighter and wipes his mouth on his sleeve. 'Out of my way, Tyler. My kidneys are bursting.'

While we wait for Garrick to return, Lily explains that yes, both he and I did imbibe a powerful drug the previous night but we did so willingly, at Professor Eardrum's party. The drug, Void, has psychotropic qualities and is thought to have potentially dangerous side-effects, but that didn't stop us. I'd love to be able to think that I'd never do such a stupid thing as this, but sadly I can make no such claim. First Brazen, now Void. I need a different hobby.

'So why did you come home with me?' I ask. 'To make sure I didn't cark it in the night?'

'Partly.'

A shadow looms over us. It's Garrick and I can see that he's back to his normal self. He's furious. 'Let's move, sister, before I decide to clamp your wheels.'

　　　GUY SALVIDGE

He ushers us out onto the blustery street, back into the horrors. The sky is leering.

—and extend a hand, slide my palm into the palm of the other. It's Lily and she's pulling me down. My lungs are bursting and I try to let go—

Eardrum's offices: a heavy door in an alleyway off Little Lonsdale Street. Lily buzzes us through into a dimly-lit reception. The door shuts behind us and I know that we have already erred. But before I can try to collar her, Lily darts off into the darkness. A brief inspection of our environs confirms that we are in a locked room. There's a reception desk but there's no one there, just like at the Ballard.

'Try that commbox one more time,' Garrick instructs me, but it won't turn on.

'Cheap-arse thing's supposed to be water resistant,' I say, rattling it. 'Where's yours?'

'I must have dropped it somewhere. Gimme a look.'

I hand it over and he studies it. 'Someone's taken out the powerpack, you schmuck. Don't tell me you let that vixen near it?' I concede that I may have allowed the vixen to touch the commbox.

'They've really got our nuts in a vice now!' he bellows, grabbing me by the collar. 'This is on your head, Seeker Bramble.' He gives me an almighty shove and I cannon into and over the reception desk. Papers go flying but they can do nothing to brake my fall. I sit up cradling my head, and there he is again.

—but she's too strong and she draws me down. Now there are other pairs of eyes and I open my mouth to scream and take in a lungful of brackish water. I lash out—

I'm on top of him and the side of his face is slicked with blood. His breath comes slow and ragged. I slide off his belly and into a crouch. 'I'm sorry,' I explain. 'Did I hit you?'

'You cracked me with your pistol,' he murmurs, 'but I'll be all right. Go finish those two. Forget about trying to make an arrest. You savvy?'

I rise woozily to my feet, ears ringing.

'We were here last night,' Garrick whispers from the floor, 'but not for a party. I sent you to arrest Eardrum. He's a pusher, Tyler. You got yourself into a tangle and had to call me for backup, remember?'

A glimmer of memory, nothing more. 'I'll get him.'

One of the internal doors clicks and I stagger over to it. I untuck my pistol from its holster, check the chamber. Six rounds. I turn the handle and kick in the door, hoping to surprise or injure anyone lurking, but there's nobody there, just a dark corridor leading to a flight of stairs.

'Come up here, Tyler,' Lily says from above. 'There's someone I'd like you to meet.' I fire blindly up into the stairwell, the sound cannoning in my ears, and begin my climb.

The door to the first floor is padlocked, but I can see a light up on the second landing. 'Don't make any sudden movements,' I warn. 'I'm pretty twitchy.'

'I'm not going to hurt you,' she says. 'Put the gun away or I won't let you in.' The door closes and I am thrown into darkness.

I reach the second floor and Lily's voice comes through an intercom: 'Lose the gun and I'll introduce you to the professor.'

'Why should I trust you?' I call through the door.

'I'm not asking you to trust me, just to play nice. All right?'

I holster it. No doubt there are surveillance cameras nearby. The door clicks and opens into another reception area. Lily is standing on the near side of the desk and the room is bright. 'Through there, please,' she says, gesturing to a particular door.

'You first,' I say. 'Open it.'

She opens it. It's an office and there's a thin, grey-haired man sitting behind the desk. He smiles bloodlessly. 'Do come in.'

My hand on the holster, I step into the room after Lily. 'You're Eardrum?' I ask.

'Eardum,' he corrects, indicating to a seat. 'Please.'

I sit facing him. Lily stands at my shoulder. I look into his sad eyes and the deep wrinkles around them.

—and her body implodes as I strike it, shrivelling to nothing. The eyes teem and multiply, illuminating this underwater cavern with their watchful gazing. I claw at them—

'You're an impulsive man, Mr Bramble. Let me salve your suffering.'

Cool hands on me, probing. I fend at them, but weakly, weakly.

'You won't be needing this any longer. Ms Fallical?'

—and they wink shut all at once, leaving me disoriented. I want to breathe, to live on, but I'm being piled upon by the heavy water. I cast about—

Naked in a bed, in a white room. Lily lays alongside me, also naked. Professor Eardum stands at the foot of the bed, syringe in hand.

His eyes bear down. 'I'm giving you a neuroleptic.'

—and spy a circle of dimness as opposed to darkness above. I thrash and it grows, lightens, and I break the surface in a surging torment. The sky is white and I am flat on my back in the catchment pool at the French fountain. The water is perhaps ten centimetres deep. I get to my feet and stand dripping in a patch of sunlight between the mighty oaks—

Lily snuggles up next to me, kisses my chest.

'What did he give me?' I ask her.

'It's the antidote, Avoid.'

'The antidote to what?'

—Garrick puffs on a cigarette. He's dripping wet himself. 'You okay, Tyler?'

'I'll live. I just slipped and hit my head is all.'

'Come on, let's get that coffee. I'm fucking freezing.'

We walk in the direction of the museum and the coffee shop within.

'What did you want to talk to me about?' I ask him.

***

See-Saw

Deborah Biancotti

'Can't do the nightshift tonight.' Sue pinched her nose between finger and thumb. 'D'I have a terrible cold.'

'It sounds rotten.'

'D'I know.'

'You should get that sorted,' Revere replied, his voice whistling with age. 'Could be a virus.'

'D'yeah.' Sue was only half-listening. Revere thought everything was a virus.

She crossed the worn carpet of her apartment and wrestled briefly with the balcony door. Then she stepped into the late afternoon.

Across the street and three storeys below she could see Mr and Mrs taking their evening stroll. Mr and Mrs ... what? Sue frowned, trying to remember their names. At least twice every day the couple toured the block. They navigated the thoroughfare with an old-fashioned perseverance, oblivious to the people around them. The busy pedestrians and the shopfront owners hawking their wares, the delivery guys who rode bikes on the footpath even though they weren't supposed to – they seemed to see none of it. For Mr and Mrs, their whole world seemed to be each other.

On the phone, Revere whistled, 'Have you got a headache?'

'Yeah.' Sue touched her fingertips to her brows. She had a headache most days. Only, it was more a hangover than a headache.

'That's bad,' Revere said.

'It is?'

Mrs was leaning on her husband's arm and Mr was tapping the street with a walking stick, striking a beat that made Mrs laugh and slap at his arm. From this distance the sounds of their progress were lost to the shouts and engines and alarms of the street. Mrs was gazing up at her husband's face, her head tipped back. A beautiful gesture but no more than that. Mrs was completely blind.

Revere said, 'How do you look?'

'What?'

Revere said it again, slower this time. 'How. Do. You. *Look*?'

Okay, that made no sense. Sue rubbed at her temples, trying to ease a new ache. Conversations with Revere did that sometimes. The guy was old but his mind was usually pretty sharp. Sharpened, maybe, by panic and pessimism – a legacy of his army days. He'd survived two world wars and still lived in a state of perpetual readiness. The apocalypse was always only about a heartbeat away.

'I look like I need some rest,' Sue muttered at last.

'I could call an ambulance?'

'Really not necessary.'

'If you're sure.' He sounded disappointed.

'Thank you, though.'

'Well. Don't you worry about a thing here, Sue. We'll keep it under control.'

Sue almost laughed. Nothing happened on the nightshift. Nothing happened and nothing ever changed.

'D'okay. Good luck with that.' She hung up the phone.

She leaned on the balcony railing and pulled her cigarettes from a pocket of her dressing gown. Mr and Mrs were still taking their stroll. There was a comfortable familiarity to their clockwork movements. Mr had hooked the walking stick over his arm so he could pat his wife's hands. It was just so darn adorable.

Sue blew smoke rings in their direction, catching the couple in a grey, hazy frame.

Mr must have caught sight of her up on her balcony, because he gave her a nod and a wave of acknowledgement. Sue nodded back and directed her smoke rings up, into the late afternoon sky.

When the couple reached the corner, Mr tapped his walking stick on the gutter and the two of them turned in a brief pirouette. They headed into an apartment block that was the mirror image of Sue's own. She lit another cigarette from the butt of the first, and traced the couple's spiralling progress up the staircase. At each landing window, Sue caught a flash of Mrs' brown coat and the silver-grey of Mr's trench.

Beauregard, that was their name.

Sue dropped the stub of her cigarette and ground it under her slipper. There was something ineffably sad about happy couples. It was like they lived in a bubble. And one way or another, bubbles always burst.

She retreated to her lounge room and the armchair where she'd dropped a packet of painkillers earlier. She swallowed two down with a glass of red and settled in to watch the twilight as it smoothed out all the edges of the world.

*

She slept for what felt like no time at all and when she woke, daylight was leaching through the balcony windows. Her headache was gone. Apart from a rumble in her stomach, Sue felt fine. Great, even. In fact, she hadn't felt this clear-headed in a long time. Like the headache had scraped out the contents of her skull and wiped it clean.

'Damn you, Revere.' She grinned. 'Scared me for no reason.'

She rubbed the grit from her eyes and leaned back, listening for some indication of the time. It must have been early, because the street below was quiet. And she was starving.

She bounced up from the armchair and into the kitchen. The fridge offered nothing, and the freezer contained only a couple of frozen dinners well past their use-by dates. She tossed one at random into the microwave. She reached for the control panel and hesitated. The clock on the microwave was a bright, scorching yellow. She squinted at it, trying to read its digits through the halo of colour. Bold, blocky numbers proclaimed the time as 6:15. It had been years since she'd seen the world at 6:15 in the morning.

She punched in the requisite seven minutes for her breakfast-dinner and rested a hip against the bench. On a whim, she switched on the kettle and made herself a cup of tea. She breathed in the steam and warmed her hands on the thick mug and felt a deep contentment for this early morning domestic ease. It was weird how good she felt.

The microwave was still counting down when a knock at the door made her jump. Hot tea burned her hand.

'Great!' Sue muttered. 'Really? At this time of day?'

The knock came again. She shook tea off her hand and crossed to the door.

A glance through the peephole revealed a lone man in a dark blue uniform. He carried a large case marked with a thick,

　　　DEBORAH BIANCOTTI

white cross. Across his left pocket, the word AMBULANCE was stencilled in yellow.

Sue swung the door wide. 'Don't tell me. Revere called.'

'If that's your boss,' the paramedic replied, 'then, yeah.'

He looked haggard. The kind of man who couldn't summon an ounce of panic.

'But I called him,' Sue said. 'I told him I wasn't coming in last night.'

The paramedic reacted as if she'd said nothing at all. 'Said he hadn't heard from you in three days. Worried it was a virus.'

'I called him yesterday. Look. I'll show you.' She pulled out her phone and worked its menu with her thumb while she held her teacup high. 'It's not a damn virus. Guy survived wars, for chrissake, why's he so—'

She stopped. There were three missed calls listed on her phone. All of them from Revere. And all of them a day apart.

'Oh. My. God,' she said. 'Three days? I've been asleep three days?'

The paramedic leaned back in an awkward arc, hands pressed to the small of his back. 'You do look pretty well rested.'

'Thanks.'

'But you should come with me, anyhow.' He leaned against the doorframe, his gaze travelling past her to the apartment behind her. She pulled the door towards her to block his view, and his gaze travelled up to her face. 'Can't leave you alone in a big place like this.'

'You're funny,' Sue said. Just to be clear, she added, 'Forget it.'

Sue began to shut the door and he stopped it with a foot. So she threw the contents of her cup in his face and when he staggered back, she shut the door. Then she locked it, just to be sure.

*

Sue paced.

'Weird. Too, too weird.'

Behind her in the kitchen, the microwave sent up a piercing bleat. It had probably been doing that for a while. Sue moved by habit, following the noise. In the kitchen, she flicked the cigarette into the sink and watched it sizzle briefly. She felt like she'd moved into a dream, where every detail was sharpened by the application of her gaze. The microwave door seemed suddenly to possess a deep lustre, and the vivid numeric display shone like the electric, amber eyes of a lion.

She touched her palm to her forehead, checking for a fever. Nothing; her skin was cool. Still, when she gazed around the kitchen, each whorl in the wood of the cupboard doors stood out, every speck on the linoleum flooring was as sharp as starlight or as deeply dark as a black hole.

'This is it,' Sue muttered. 'I'm finally going nuts.'

The morning sky outside the balcony revealed nothing about the day or date, nothing that indicated that anything was different or strange. But the quiet of the early morning was enduring. The traffic was silent, the voices of shop owners calling their trade was inaudible. You couldn't tell Thursday from Sunday on this street. It was always the same.

She located the cigarettes, now crumpled, in her pocket and selected the least bent one. Then she lit it with trembling fingers and took a long, long breath. She dropped ash in her empty cup. She'd never smoked inside before. It felt wrong. She took the cigarette to the balcony. Mr and Mrs Beauregard were outside, taking an early morning stroll. Mrs held her husband's arm tight to her chest. Mr tapped the ground with his borrowed cane.

She took another drag on the cigarette. Mrs was talking, her hands pressed to her husband's arm. Mr put his head back and laughed, and in that instant he must have seen Sue up on her balcony. He gave her a familiar nod. Sue sucked on her cigarette and gazed down at him through the smoke. She felt numb.

Mr frowned and then raised his hand in a wave. *All okay?* he seemed to be asking. Sue hesitated. Maybe the fear was showing up in her face. She raised her own hand in a thumbs-up gesture. Then she pressed her fingertips to the bridge of her nose, trying to smooth the frown that had taken hold. Maybe she really was coming down with something. She'd certainly never felt this *weird* before. Mr looked puzzled, but soon the couple moved on.

Sue ground out her cigarette and stood with her eyes closed, fingers pressed to her temples. She focused on breathing, trying to force some calm into her locked skull.

The air was warm and sweet at this time of the morning. Unusually warm and sweet. In fact, not like city air at all. More like the finest air in the world had been pumped in from just

   DEBORAH BIANCOTTI

outside the manor houses of some distant countryside. She opened her eyes.

'What. The. *Hell*?'

The city sidewalk was gone. The whole city was gone. The shopfronts had been replaced with a tree-lined laneway, and the apartment block opposite her own – the one Mr and Mrs lived in – had become a tall mansion with gardens either side, a wide, round driveway in front, and arched windows on all its four floors.

Sue let out a low whistle. The place was beautiful, with an old-fashioned charm that reminded her of the Beauregards themselves. It was beautiful, but it was wrong. Mr appeared at the windows then, pulling them apart so he could step through. He tilted his face to the morning sun. The morning light eased the wrinkles from his skin. He looked young. Sue raised a hand to wave, but his eyes were closed.

Mrs appeared beside him. She drew the curtains open, fixing them to each side of the glass panes so they hung in heavy folds. In all the time Sue had watched the Beauregards, she'd never seen Mrs anywhere but on her husband's arm. Now she turned and patted his elbow and Sue realised there was an accuracy to the way she adjusted the curtains and led her husband from the window. An accuracy that a blind woman might struggle with in a brand new house, in a brand new world.

Sue turned back into her apartment. She moved past the expansive lounge suite and the ornate armoire her sister had bought her, the one with inlays of rosewood and—

'Rosewood?'

Sue didn't even know what rosewood was. Come to think of it, she wasn't sure what an armoire was and she sure as hell had never owned one. On top of that, she didn't have a sister. She turned to it. The armoire – if it was one – had tall, pointed doors that fitted together snugly and a brocade tassel that hung from a handle. There was a dense familiarity to it, like it belonged there. Like it had spent years in her apartment. Except this apartment looked a heck of a lot better than the one she remembered waking up in. The worn carpet had been replaced with patterned rugs over parquetry floors. The furniture was ornate and plush. The walls were painted in rich colours to reflect the artwork that hung under spotlights.

'Okay. That is totally not my artwork,' Sue muttered.

She thought back to the Beauregards in their giant mansion. Then she turned and ran for the door. The room seemed to stretch and grow around her. She ran faster, first to the wide front door and then out, into the thickly-planted lane outside her house.

'My *house*?'

There was nothing outside but grass and trees and more grass and trees, and across the way, the mansion that had grown up around Mr and Mrs. She jogged towards their door. The door handle was an elaborate hound's head in rich ironwork. She rapped once, sending up a booming echo that must have been audible throughout the mansion. The door swung majestically open.

'Mr—'

'Hello?' It was Mrs, looking right at her with eyes that were clear and bright.

'Mrs ... ?'

'Yes?' Mrs smiled.

'Beauregard?'

'That's right.'

Sue said, 'I live across the road, in the apartment block. Only ... You can totally see me, can't you?'

'Ah.' Mrs smiled more brightly. 'You better come inside.'

She gestured Sue in, since the door was already wide open and the hallway behind her was spacious enough for a small circus to set up a tent. Sue stepped forward, keeping her back to the wall, looking at the animated face of Mrs. There was a movement further along the hallway and Mr appeared. He walked with one hand to the wall. His face was dazed and his eyes were pale and blank.

'Oh, no,' Sue said. 'Now *he's* blind?'

Mr said, 'Who is it, dear?'

'It's me, Mr Beauregard,' Sue said. 'I live in the apartment across the road. We often wave hello.'

'We do?' Mr smiled, his face angled away from her. He came towards her, trailing his fingers along the patterned wallpaper. 'Ah, yes. Suzanne, isn't it?'

'Sue.' It had never been Suzanne.

Mr reached out a hand to his wife and she took it in her own,

          DEBORAH BIANCOTTI

curling her fingers through his. Mrs smiled up at him.

'Tea?' he offered.

'We can take it in the library,' Mrs replied.

Then she swung the front door shut behind them, blocking out the strange world Sue had travelled across.

Mr volunteered to make the tea. Sue watched him turn and trail his hand along the wall, in the apparent direction of the kitchen.

Mrs leaned in. 'I'm afraid our tea might take a while. Mr Beauregard refuses to accept any help. He's so very proud.'

'He's blind,' Sue said.

'Yes, dear.'

'That makes no sense.'

Mrs hesitated. 'I think you need to sit down.'

'I sure do,' Sue agreed.

Mrs looped her arm through Sue's and pulled her forward. She manoeuvred them into a room to the right of the hall. The walls were lined with books and there were three broad leather lounges in the middle of a plush rug.

'It's beautiful,' Sue said.

'Isn't it?'

'And it's impossible.'

Mrs laughed. She took a seat on one of the lounges and gestured Sue to another. 'You must be wondering what's going on.'

'You got that right.' Sue took the offered seat, curling herself into a corner of the lounge. 'Everything's changed, everything's—'

'Better?'

'Exactly.'

'Not everything.' Mrs smiled. She took a breath and clasped her hands in her lap. 'When I was blind, I relied on my husband to describe the world to me. And what he described ... It seemed so beautiful. It seemed just like this, actually.'

'He lied to you, then.'

Mrs raised an instructive finger and tapped the air with it. 'He embellished.'

'He was good at it.'

'Yes. He was.'

'And you believed him?'

'Of course not.' Mrs clasped her hands in front of her. 'You know, when I was blind—'

'Yeah, what happened to that?'

'When I was blind,' Mrs continued, 'my husband built me a new world, I guess you could say. A place that was safe and wonderful to live in. A place inside the real world.'

'A bubble,' Sue muttered.

'Well, bubbles burst, dear.'

'Don't they just?'

'This might not. This might be forever.'

Sue hesitated. 'Will it, though?'

She wanted to add *please* to that question. Will it *please* last forever? Will it *please* be the real world now?

'I mean,' Sue continued, 'what if it's a virus?'

'A virus?' Mrs looked confused.

Sue shrugged.

'I don't think it's a virus.'

'No. Probably not.'

'Why would it be a virus?' Mrs persisted.

'Look, it's just something I heard.'

'If it is, I do hope there's no cure.'

'Okay.'

Mrs slapped a palm against the coffee table. 'People pathologise everything. Any kind of change or difference, it must be a sickness. Any—'

'All right already.' Sue raised both hands in surrender.

Mrs sighed and leaned back. She cast a look towards the corridor where her husband had disappeared. She seemed thoughtful and maybe a little sad. 'Whatever it is, we should enjoy it while it lasts. Shouldn't we, dear?'

'I suppose.' Sue shrugged.

'I mean it's all we can do.'

Sue wrapped her arms around her knees and hunkered deeper into the lounge that shouldn't exist.

From the doorway, Mr appeared bearing a tray of teacups. Mrs stood and moved to him, guiding him by the elbow until he was able to place the tray on a low table in the middle of the lounges. Mr Beauregard touched unpractised fingers to the cups. He reached for the teapot and accidentally knocked a cup in its saucer. He laughed and Mrs joined him, straightening the cup between her husband's fingers.

Sue ran her hands along the cool leather. She looked at the fine

     DEBORAH BIANCOTTI

china cups with their steaming, warm tea. She looked at last at
the faces of her neighbours, soft and serene with the sunlight
from the windows gilding their chins and hair.

'You know,' Sue said, watching them.

'Yes, dear?' said Mr.

Sue leaned forward to accept a cup of tea. 'I guess I'll see how
it goes.'

***

Bluey and Myrtle

Mark O'Flynn

'Who's a pretty boy, then?'
  'Who's a pretty boy, then?'
  'Give us a kiss.'
  'Give us a kiss.'
  'Who's a pretty boy?'
  I'm the pretty boy. No one else. Pretty Bluey. Me. My pretty plumage.
  'Who loves his Mummy, then?'
  'Who loves his Mummy, then?'
  'Who's been making a great big mess?'
  That's going too far. Yes, I repudiate that. Pretty is as pretty does.

*

Three thousand six hundred and fifty-three days, but who's counting? I'm getting on. Each morning like this one, the same beginning. The same light bulb burning brightly in the ceiling. How have we come to this?
  Myrtle.
  Myrtle's eyes vast and rheumy behind her glasses. She places a sunflower seed between her lips and presses her face up against the wires of the cage. Her lips make a plastic smooching noise, pursed around the seed like an anus. Pretty Bluey knows all about simile and metaphor. I used to read the newspapers spread out on the table below, over the shoulder of the old fellow. He was a great one for the crosswords. She expects me to bounce on my perch, bob my head, and take the seed from between her lips. I do. It's a kind of frigid, bestial kiss.
  This is morning.

*

She scratches the cere of my beak with a fingernail. I hold the seed in my claw and examine it. I crack it open and nibble the kernel. Stale. What does she expect, a thank-you?
  'Give us a kiss,' she says.
  'Give us a kiss,' I reply.

                         MARK O'FLYNN

It doesn't matter how I say the words, I don't have to mean them. It's echolalia. She fills my seed tray and water bowl too. The same water bowl, all these years. Her giant hand squeezing in through the tiny gate. I grip the dowel rod of the perch as the cage rocks. My mirror and bell swing wildly on their chain, creating the illusion of cheerful, if fragmented company. Ha! When once it swung on its umbilicus of string, Twitters, my mate, was so offended by its patronising attempt to create a society for us that he pecked through the thread and let it fall. Myrtle hooked it back up with an old watch chain, so now it twirls forever of its own accord, swinging in the breeze, reflecting a spasm of sunlight. Unless it was the old fellow who hooked it back up. It was from his watch.

*

'Doesn't Bluey like his breakfast?' Myrtle says.

I deign to reply. *For God's sake, Myrtle, put the cover back on. It's torture.* I squawk rudely. The bouncing sun dazzles my eyes at random moments. She doesn't understand. She thinks it affectionate play when I peck at the little mirror, when in reality I am trying to rip my own impostor's eyes out. Each morning, when the cover is removed, the sudden galaxy of the kitchen is a shock to my delicate system. It's too big; too noisy when she bangs about in the cupboards after the sinister peace of the night. I'm all on edge when she clatters amongst the saucepans looking for something she cannot find, muttering, muttering.

Myrtle, put the cover back on; go back to bed; put us both out of our misery.

*

At dusk she comes to arrange the frilly curtain (she made it herself) over the dome of my cage. It's hardly an aviary, although when Twitters was alive, yes, yes, *this perch thy centre was, these bars thy spheare.* We'd splash in the dish and flap water out onto the crosswords below. No happier pair of lovebirds could you find, discussing all the issues of the day. (*Oh, Twitters.*) She used to let us out, one at a time, to flutter about the wide open skies of the kitchen. Perch on the curtain rods. Or else on her finger. Once Twitters banged into the window pane. Lord how I squawked. We saw the mynah birds in their robbers' masks outside the window, bullying the sparrows. Ruling the roost. Noisy miscreants. In turn we flew ecstatic circles around the light shade. If only she had let us both out at once, escape might have been feasible. Once the old fellow came in unexpectedly and his snowy hair looked right for nesting material, but that was just instinct.

'Quickly, Alf, shut the door.'

'Jesus, they're loose.'

'Only one is loose. I'm training them.'

'What for, combat?'

What a terrible glimpse of freedom that was; that chasm of possibility. Did Twitters contemplate it? For one to leave the other and cross the threshold. It was unthinkable. So we returned dutifully to our coop, wing muscles stiffening after exercise, glad, it must be said, to be home. Mandela's cell was much bigger when he lived in it.

*

Until one day – that tragic day – I woke to find Twitters' tiny heart had given up the ghost and he had dropped off his perch. Diminished and flat in the sawdust at the bottom of the cage. I'll never forget poor Myrtle's face when she came to remove the cover and saw my love, cold and shrivelled on the floor; the rictus of his beak; his claws gripped as if around a seed. She nearly had a fit. *18 across, 10 letters: abolition of sudden diminution of sensation and voluntary motion* – what could that be? Pencil scratching at the temple – *apoplectic.* No other word for it. Poor duck. Like that too when she found the old fellow.

*

From that day on, I took it on myself to rid the cage of every death-infected scrap of sawdust that she persists in shovelling into my habitat. My world. Not hers. With great diligence, I scratch and flick them out between the bars at night. It has become part of the ritual. Dawn comes. The alarm rings. Her curtains rattle open. She hobbles down stairs with the pot. Empties it in the lav. Gives it a rinse. She fills the kettle. She gets the milk from the fridge. All these things I know, with the extra sensory perception of the blind, even before she whips the

MARK O'FLYNN

floral shroud off the cage. *Squawk!* The glaring, naked bulb. Or else the piercing eastern sun.

'Who's a pretty boy, then?'

Her great, nude irises, paling with age.

'Come on, Bluey. Who's a pretty boy, then?'

I take my head from under my wing, make the reply: *whistle, squawk, chirrup.*

'Who's been making a great big mess, then?'

'Great big mess.'

She fetches the dustpan and brush from beneath the sink and sweeps up the contaminated shavings. I must say that apart from my obsessive compulsion I rather like the look of the flakes as they float gently down through the moonlight. And the breast feathers I have torn out with my own beak and tossed overboard. I am the life-giving pelican drawing its own blood to feed its young. But there are no young. There is no one.

16 across, 4 letters: ego; the focus of solipsism - - - - sacrifice.

*

Cover off. Light on. Day begun. I watch Myrtle at her rituals. She takes the kettle off the stove and fills the teapot. Twirls it three times. The milk. The strainer. The careful pouring. The dreadful humanity of it. It took her a long time to learn she only needed one cup. *Chirp chirp chirp.* I'm here, too. Without each other, old girl, where are we?

'Who's a pretty boy, then?' I try to encourage her, but she seems distracted this morning. Instead of putting the kettle back on the stove she puffs out the flame like a candle, puts the kettle on the table. The milk bottle goes in a cupboard. That look on her face, she's trying to remember something, like a word on the tip of her tongue. Someone's birthday. Whose can it be? I gaze down on her grey curls. Myrtle, Myrtle (I want to shriek), let's set aside this grieving we've both grown so used to. The bald and bleeding patch on my breast throbs where I have dug out the roots of my quills. Something in my whistle alerts her. Despair perhaps. She comes to stare through the wire. The fading cerulean blue of her eyes. Sometimes, when the mirror spins, I understand that it is only me whom I glimpse in dizzy reflection; yet part of me could swear that I am not alone, and it is Twitters, my love, risen off the floor, returned to me.

What a mystery, the apperception of consciousness.

*

Myrtle presses her lips to the bars. Her face is near.

'Who's a pretty boy?'

Squaaaawk! Twitters. Twitters was the pretty boy. A downright flirt. I wonder if I have time to peck out an eye? No. She's fast for an old duck.

Her tea. Her breakfast. Her washing up. I can't go on, so I suppose I'll go on.

'Oh my goodness, Bluey, you haven't had your muesli.'

I have, Myrtle. I have. Look. Don't you remember? She'll forget me altogether one day. Just as she's forgotten to turn the gas off. Listen, hissing steadily from the ring. Chirp. Heroic deeds of Bluey the mining canary, asphyxiated in the line of patriotic duty. I could have told her you don't blow out the flame like a birthday candle. She calls the mishmash she gives me 'muesli'. The old fellow used to laugh at that. It was his job to mix the sesame and sunflower seeds in an empty jam tin, to lift the little gate with his great hairy fingers, as Myrtle does now, to slide the saucer of seed in through the aperture. She baulks when she sees that my tray is already full.

'Oh dear,' she says. 'Aren't you hungry?'

No, I'm not hungry. The open gate is a guillotine, stoppered up by her hand. She takes out the still full dish and replaces it with another full dish.

'Now, Bluey, what was I looking for? I suppose I'll remember when I find it.'

Myrtle turns back to the sink. The gate is open. Stuck at the top. All those hideous mynah birds in the branches outside the windows. There are more of them these days. Murderous fecundity. The kitchen is frightening enough. I could casually flop down from my perch, peck at the seed, as on any normal morning, give a spontaneous gargle of song, before tugging down on the gate, as Twitters used to do when Myrtle forgot to close it, so we were safe again. I call out.

'Myrtle, Myrtle, shut the gate.'

I could say anything, she wouldn't hear. She's busy doing the dishes. Humming. She's forgotten me. There's a whole day to get through. No one ever bothers to visit anymore.

 MARK O'FLYNN

But there's something about this morning, something about the fundamental limitations of language as a means of communication between two sentient beings.

'Myrtle the turtle,' I squawk. 'You've left the gas on. *Poo-tee-weet!*'

I smell the gas rising. Thick and fast. It won't be long now, Twitters. I suppose, like me, she has her own memories of the old fellow. The look on her face when she came in to find him on the kitchen floor beneath us, the new bulb in his hand, an Osram from memory, the step ladder on its side. Sparks everywhere. *18 across, 10 letters*. No muesli that day, I can tell you. Nor, a year later, when Twitters was removed in a tissue. In a tissue, for God's sake! Cold as a frog. His legs pitifully thin compared to the rest of him. Christ only knows what happened after that. No, it's Myrtle and me. And she's left the gas on. And the trapdoor open. The stove hissing softly in the corner like a bronchial lung. Listen, Myrtle, I don't want to pine away up here forever, why don't you buy another pretty boy to keep me company; some handsome, androgynous *Melopsittacus undulatus*, with green tail feathers, for preference. I'll teach him how to speak real proper like.

*

I hop down from my perch. Ruffle my wings. Scratch myself.
  'Who's a pretty boy, then?'
  'Who's a pretty boy, then?' she answers.
  'I am, Myrtle, I am.'
  She doesn't skip a beat. Dish, fork, plate, knife, spoon, bowl.
  'And who made a great big mess, then?'
  'I did, Myrtle, I did.'
I nibble the seed. I stretch my otiose wings. They make a noise like flags on a windy day. Small flags, I admit, flapping in the winds of destiny. I see the open window beyond the open cage. The yellow masks of mynah birds in the trees outside. Myrtle is humming. A bee in her bonnet that she doesn't know is there. Dish, fork, plate, knife, spoon, bowl. She's washing the same cutlery that she's washed already. I stand beneath the rusted door. I will it to drop, but it is not heavy and would probably only give me a clonk on the beak. Fate is beckoning, or is it opportunity? I take off.

Freedom. *Flap flap flap.*

'Oh, Bluey, Bluey, come back,' Myrtle squawks, dropping the dish mop.

I circumnavigate the airspace of the kitchen.

Cheep.

'Come back, you naughty bird.'

I perch on the curtain rod. Morning ablution down the drapes.

'Oh, Bluey.'

I buzz the kitchen. Strafe the dishes. The gas is thicker up near the ceiling. I'm a raptor! Bank away from the open window. The mynahs are watching the whole charade. Plenty of dust up here on the cupboards where she can't reach anymore. I soar. I glide. I loop-the-loop. My stunted wings clip the hot Osram in the socket of the ceiling. It must be loose for, surprisingly, it plummets to the floor. Newton's light bulb. I watch it plummet as if in slow motion. Down, down. Shatters on the lino with a soft pop, making Myrtle jump. Thin slivers of glass, like fish scales, scatter under the fridge and stove. The room darkens appreciatively. I swoop.

'Come back, Bluey.'

'Not on your life. I'm free! *Poo-tee-weet.*'

What does she want? You give a chap language and then expect subservience? God did not decree that consciousness be solely of the human sphere. *Anthropoavian*, surely that's a crossword clue.

'Oh, Bluey, what a mess.'

'You bet, sister.'

I swoop again. I chirp my heart out. I am faced with the open window or the empty cage. In or out. Zenith versus nadir. It's not often I really get to think about these paradoxes. About where I belong. *Ask, rather, what the universe has done to deserve me?* Where the light bulb has fallen from the ceiling, the socket is open and exposed. The switch by the door is still on. As it was when the old fellow was still with us. He wouldn't listen when Twitters warned him to dry his hands first. Cause and effect. First law of electrical conductivity. I'm coming, Twitters. The temptation is too great. I swoop. I soar. A phoenix risen from the sawdust. Blaze of glory. Sparks everywhere. Socket open. Up through the gas I rise on eagle's wings unto the flowering hypothesis of Heaven.

 MARK O'FLYNN

The Rift

Chris Somerville

A month after I'm back and Dad says that it's going to be me who puts down one of the horses. He's been getting me to do odd jobs in exchange for living at home. I don't complain about having to shoot Peppercorn, even though I can tell Dad wants me to. We're at the table in the living room and he tilts back in his chair and stares at me, not blinking.

If we ever have to do anything official like this he makes me sit at the table across from him, like he's my boss. He used to do this when he worked over at the quarry, back when people still worked there.

'It won't be that hard, I'm sure you killed a lot of them over there,' Mum says.

'She means towelheads,' Dad says. 'Not ponies.'

I go to explain that it's different, but then there'd probably be more questions afterwards. Since coming back I've discovered I could just keep quiet about things and people would nod at me in a knowing way, acting like they could read my mind.

I say, 'All right then.'

'The poor thing,' Mum says.

'He's in a lot of pain at the moment,' Dad says. 'It's better this way.'

What happened: the three horses all stampeded earlier in the morning and Peppercorn fell in a dried-out creek bed and broke two legs. I don't like to think about it, since I've always liked him more than the other horses. After he's dead Dad reverses a forklift in to the stable to pick him up. It beeps while he does this and it feels like the only sound for miles.

*

The next morning Mum makes pancakes. I think it's on account of me shooting my favourite horse, but I always have a hard time guessing at what she's thinking. When I came back home she made macaroni and cheese for dinner, which she knows is my favourite, but then she served it up again one week later, so who knows.

'Do you want sugar and lemon or just maple syrup?' she says.

'Syrup,' I say.

'It's imitation but I don't think people can really tell the difference,' she says.

After I've eaten I borrow her car to go see Jeremy, who also lives with his parents but in town. When we were in high school we were in a band together, with me on drums and Jeremy on guitar, but then I joined the army and that kind of broke the band up and I'm not sure what we are anymore. He had a good voice. We used to make a pretty big racket.

I get a headache while driving. When I'm in Jeremy's house I ask him for some Panadol and he pours me a glass of water and searches through the kitchen drawers. This is the second time I've seen him since coming back.

'I'm sure we keep some in here,' he says.

'It'll pass if not,' I say, because I don't want him to make a big deal out of things. Since I last saw him he's gotten thicker and let his hair grow long, but he still has the same voice, the same bedroom in his parents' house. Whenever he goes to speak his mouth still turns downwards, like he's about to start yelping.

'If they're not in here then I can't think where I've left them,' Jeremy says. 'I've been awake since early morning. Cooper's run off.'

'Who's that?' I say.

'My dog.'

I shake my head and try to look sympathetic, but Jeremy's not really watching me. I tell him to get up, since he's on his knees down on the kitchen floor, rummaging. I say, 'It's not that bad anyway.'

'Is it from gunfire?' Jeremy says.

'I don't think so,' I say. 'I shot a horse yesterday.'

Jeremy gives me a funny look and then I'm thinking that maybe I've said the wrong thing. I shrug at him. I've never seen his dog before, not even a photograph.

'I can drive you around?' I offer. 'He'll probably turn up.'

*

In Mum's car Jeremy makes all these minor adjustments while I drive. To his seat and to the air conditioning. He pulls at things

            CHRIS SOMERVILLE

like he's testing to see how much is broken.

'I think it's funny that of all the places to come back to, you chose this one,' Jeremy says.

'It's hilarious,' I agree.

'You know what I mean,' he says.

I do know what he means. Ours is not a very large town, there's one main street with a church and a post office and a supermarket. On weekends we'd go and hang out in the car park of the supermarket, or sometimes on the steps of the church. Mum has been getting on at me about what I plan to do now that I'm back and all I can ever offer her is a shrug.

I'm not sure if I'm supposed to be here anymore. I drive up the main strip, get to the end, and then turn back around. There's a few people shopping and walking around and Jeremy nods at all of them. I'd probably recognise their names if they introduced themselves. The people here are okay, but even Jeremy, who's the closest thing I have to a best friend, has his own name tattooed on his forearm, like he'll forget.

I pull in behind the supermarket and turn the engine. It's a cold day and the clouds above us are huge, motionless. There's a silence in town that makes my jaw ache. I wonder how long it's been since I've had quiet like this. Even at Mum and Dad's place I hardly ever hear a bird.

'What now?' Jeremy says.

'I want some soda water,' I say. 'Let's continue our search on foot.'

*

As far as I can see there's only warm soda water sitting on the shelves in the supermarket. I'm trying to find someone who works there to help me out when I run into my old neighbour, Mrs Bell, who lived across the street from us until we had to move out of town. I don't have a memory of ever meeting Mr Bell, though she used to talk of him like he was there.

'You're back,' she says.

'I am,' I say.

'That's quite surprising,' she says. 'I didn't think they'd have let you out.'

'No it was all okay,' I say, a little confused. 'I signed the discharge papers and everything.'

Jeremy comes by us, carrying a large sausage made for dogs. It's wrapped up tight in blue plastic with a metal clip at the top. It looks like a balloon.

He says, 'I figure if we drive around with this hanging out of the window, Cooper's bound to come home.'

'You should leave a sign out the front,' Mrs Bell says. 'That's what I've been telling everyone else.'

She says this while looking at me in a way I don't appreciate. Something like hatred or wariness or even straight-up fear. I knew a guy like that in my unit who eventually flicked a knife into the ground at my feet and spat at me and said we were going to get this done. He'd hit me a few times, but I'd managed to sweep his legs out from under him and get him on his back and I had to be pulled off of him in the end, otherwise I don't think I would have stopped.

In the supermarket I'm suddenly aware of how I'm breathing, like there isn't enough air getting in to my head. I go to the checkout and buy the warm soda water and the dog sausage and make Jeremy leave with me, all the time saying as little as possible to anyone.

*

Out the front of the supermarket we look at the community board. There are paper fliers all over it, some even stapled around its frame. When a breeze comes the whole thing flutters like a tree.

'That's ridiculous,' I say. 'Doesn't anyone clean these up?'

'They're all new,' Jeremy says. 'All of them.' He's sounding more glum than usual.

I look closer. They're not just for dogs, I notice, although there are a lot of them missing. Spotty, Jaffa, Zoe, all vanished. There are cats too, and even a few horses. One cow. I recognise a few of the family names written on the bottom of the fliers, along with phone numbers, some email addresses.

'I've seen this kind of thing before, but for people, children. In neighbourhoods and near schools, close to where we'd been bombing.

'Surely they can't have all left together?' Jeremy says.

'No,' I say. 'That wouldn't make any sense.'

                    CHRIS SOMERVILLE

Mrs Bell has followed us out, and she's gathered a small crowd behind her from the supermarket. I count about seven people. Two of them are dressed like they work here, in black vests, white shirts.

'This is what I meant,' Mrs Bell says.

'It's staggering,' I say.

'That's not what I mean,' she says.

I only have to look at her properly to know what she means now. When I was twelve, we moved out of town after I took Dad's rifle down to the park, rested the barrel on a tree branch, and shot a dog that Mr Johnson, my principal, was walking, to get some exercise in before work. For a while everyone talked about it, and maybe they still do. I hadn't been home in a while.

I look around, at Jeremy who's looking away from me, at the people who have crowded around me.

'I didn't mean to shoot that dog,' I say. 'I didn't know that would happen back then. I was a lot dumber than I am now.'

'Who's to say you didn't kill all these ones too?' Mrs Bell says.

She's saying this while pointing at me. This makes me mad for two reasons. The first being that I hadn't killed Mr Johnson's dog in the first place, only winged it in its hind quarters, and it's still alive today as far as I know. The second is that judging by the amount of dogs gone, at least fifty, not to mention the cats and horses and cow, there was no way I could have pulled off this kind of operation.

I go to explain this, but then one of the checkout guys comes towards me, and it's like I'm back in the desert – I sweep his leg out and I'm on top of him hitting his face, until Jeremy comes and pulls me off. Everyone is standing around, not doing anything, and the kid's on the ground, groaning, with blood coming out of his nose and mouth.

I realise then that he's probably only about sixteen. I think about helping him up but then decide not to touch anyone ever again, and anyway Jeremy still has his hand on my shoulder, pulling me away.

*

I let Jeremy drive us back, but it's such a short trip from town to his house that I don't have time to tell him anything on the way. When he pulls into his driveway he gets out and leaves the engine running. I tell him that I hope Cooper comes back but I don't think he hears me and he's even left the dog sausage sitting on the back seat. I think about leaning back and securing it with a seatbelt as a joke, but it doesn't feel very funny.

Back in basic you used to be able to hear the field they used for artillery training, and it would be a dull roar all day, like a storm rolling in that got snagged and was just sitting out there, waiting to flatten you. I could dream the sound so well sometimes that I'd wake up thinking I was back there.

I can hear this sound on my drive back home, back down our driveway, back past the patch of dirt where Peppercorn is buried.

I'm thinking: *I shouldn't have told Jeremy about shooting that horse.*

*

Mum answers the phone when the sun's coming down. I can tell from how quiet she's speaking that the phone call is about me. She looks at me nervously, like I'm ready to explode. I look over at Dad, who's sitting in his chair with his glasses on, doing a crossword in a newspaper that he's folded over again and again until it's firm enough to support his pen.

I say, 'I'm going to get in trouble.'

'Why?' he says. 'What did you do now?'

'I hit someone in town. He might have been a kid.'

'With the car?'

'With my hands.'

'What do you mean might have been a kid?'

I look at Dad square in the eye for a moment to try and guess what he's thinking about. Mum's standing in the doorway.

'He was too big to tell,' I say. 'He surprised me.' Then I get up and head outside, careful not to slam the door behind me, in case they mistake me for being angry.

Outside I walk around our paddock, waiting for the sun to vanish so it can wipe out the rest of today. I can hear the horses going nuts in their stable. I decide that I hate this whole place. What happened to the rest of my friends from here? Bill Winston moved for work. Robert Lax fell from a ladder trying

     CHRIS SOMERVILLE

to fix his TV reception and broke his neck. Stephen Carney killed himself by filling a glass of water with enough aspro to make it as thick as wall plaster.

Others drifted away; the ones I knew only by their Christian name or surname, but never both. Not as far as I can remember.

*

I'm trying to recall all of these people when I see a dog. It's moving along our fence line at the back of our property, where the trees are thicker and the land starts to climb up to the ridge. It's an Alsatian and it's loping along in a carefree manner. It looks at me once when I start following it, but doesn't quicken its pace or slow down. It doesn't care about me at all.

We travel onwards and up the ridge, heading back towards town, but above it. The higher we get the more I can see. I'm with the dog now, we've both slowed, and now and then I rest my hand on its back while we walk. We're both out of breath. By the time we make it to the top of the ridge I'm beat and I stop, with my arms resting on my knees. From where I am I can make out the church and the post office and have a guess at where Jeremy's house is, though I don't know exactly.

The Alsatian has stopped beside me now, waiting.

'Give me a moment,' I say, though I don't like to talk to animals like they're regular people because it makes me feel dumb.

Below us on the side opposite to town, there's a small expanse of thin bushland, and then the quarry, which I'd thought would be empty but I can see things moving around inside it. I stare for a while before I work out that I can see horses down there, and dogs sitting in packs. They're hard to make out exactly, but now and then one of them will get up from where they're sitting and move around.

I make the Alsatian sit, which he does obediently, but then he starts to howl. I tell him to stop but he doesn't. Back in town I can see all the lights going off, all at once. There's the dog howling and then the other dogs start up too, down in the quarry.

'Quiet down,' I say to the dog. 'Shut your mouth.'

The first thing I see collapsing is the church. It looks like it's happening slowly at first, but then the steeple hits the ground and then the ground falls away and nothing is left there, not even a cloud of dust. Then the post office goes too, the streets cave in. There's also the supermarket and the houses around town and the whole street where Jeremy's house was – it all gets swallowed up into the ground. The cave moves outward and dark, like someone knocked over a giant bottle of ink, and really what I'm thinking about is how quiet it all is. I can see my house and the rift moving towards it and then it's swallowed up too, Mum and Dad and even dead and buried Peppercorn. The Alsatian keeps howling by my side until I place my hand on the back of its head.

He shuts up then and so there's nothing else, just silence.

****

    CHRIS SOMERVILLE

Hare

Carmel Bird

The Facts

Ginny Peach was shot dead in her studio. It happened in the early hours of the morning following the opening of her show *Morning Hare.* A single bullet to the head. Six of the paintings, all pictures of hares, some black, some white, some red, some accompanied by the blurred figure of a titian-haired woman, had also been shot. The hares all had holes between the eyes. Somebody was a very good shot. The paintings resembled in style, a little, the work of Arthur Boyd. Everybody said that. The price went up after the shooting, but that was no use to Ginny.

She must have known her killer, the police said, since there was no evidence of forced entry. Such is the useful language of a police investigation – *killer, forced entry.* The weapon was a hunting rifle. All this took place in the bush on the outskirts of the Victorian city of Bendigo, in Santa Monica Gully.

It didn't take long for the police to make their way to the home of Dan Tasco, a twenty-minute drive from Ginny's studio down a rough bush track. He was taken in for questioning – more useful language – and before long was charged with murder. They never found the rifle.

What can have possessed him, people wondered. He had been his usual self at the opening, Ginny's good friend and neighbour. You just never know, do you. Of course, he had never really been the same since his wife died – well, disappeared. Mad with grief some people said. Others whispered that he had – as it were – done away with her. A wide area had been searched, police descending into the earth where dangerous old gold mines offered possibilities and secrets. It was a good five years since all that happened, and there was no fresh evidence, although the case was naturally still very much open.

A week or so after Dan was charged regarding Ginny's death, he wrote a rambling confession that would answer people's questions, up to a point, but would pose deeper mysteries of its own. There would be many mysteries, seemingly related. Intertwined. Were they? Unanswered questions. Dan said he couldn't recall what he had done with the gun. He didn't remember going to the studio or going home. But he knew he shot Ginny Peach. He said she had it coming, *obviously*, he said. Why? She just did. It was obvious.

It was clear that Dan was not his usual easygoing self. They searched the dam at the bottom of the hill on Dan's property. Again. Five years earlier divers had done all that. Looking for a body. To no avail. His lawyer – it was Elizabeth McGee from the old firm of *McGee and Moffet* in Bendigo – had advised him most strongly against writing the confession, but Dan insisted he had to get everything off his chest.

Elizabeth was an old girlfriend. She knew him very well. She said what he wrote was too wild and out of control, even though it did contain the confession about the shooting.

Poor Dan, she thought, marrying that loopy Arielle. Elizabeth actually believed he hadn't done the shooting. Ginny had plenty of enemies about the place, and it could have been any of them. Persons unknown.

No, Elizabeth said, Dan didn't do it. No, he's not himself, not his usual self, but this thing doesn't add up. He couldn't have done it, it just wasn't in him to do a thing like that, and where is the gun? First find the rifle. And how did he get from his farm to the studio and back in the time-frame when his ute was on blocks? A mate had driven him to the opening and back. It made no sense. That's what Elizabeth said.

*

Dan Tasco's Confession
My late wife Arielle – well, I say 'late wife', but in fact there is no real guarantee she's dead. Missing. Arielle is missing. I understand that Ginny's dead. Yes, she's dead all right. That's quite straightforward. They found Arielle's iPod in the scrub near the old Starlight mine – defunct of course, the mine. The only thing on the iPod was somebody reading *Wuthering Heights*. I could have told them that. She was crazy about that book. She's been missing for nearly five years now. I think of her as dead, you know. I dream about her lovely long red hair. Titian. It's one of those stories – a woman sets out in the early morning light to go for a walk in the bush. She did this walk just about every day, ever since we moved here to the central goldfields and started growing the sunflowers. *Rivers and fields*

 CARMEL BIRD

of pure gold, Arielle said. She was poetic. She sets out in the early morning light. Never comes home. You hear about people who go missing and clear off to Sydney and start a whole new life with a new family and a job in IT or something. Or else they end up in a shallow grave just off the highway somewhere, and their bodies are traced by the smart phones in their jeans. Easy. But Arielle never had a smart phone. She didn't even have an email address. She sometimes used the laptop to send emails via my address, but not very often. She was, as maybe her name suggests, a bit airy-fairy, not down to earth, dreamy. Well, like I said, she was poetic, spiritual. Vulnerable actually. Even more tuned in to unreality I reckon, since baby William died from cot death. We tried for another baby, but nothing happened. Our sex life was OK, but no baby. That was a year before Arielle disappeared, the cot death. You know. Naturally the police, once they had decided to take my report of her being missing seriously, wanted to study her emails on my laptop for clues to her 'disappearance'. They didn't find anything particularly useful, I have to say. There were messages to her so-called friend Ginny Peach – just down the road – a forty-minute walk. I will have more to say about Ginny in due course. Obviously. I shot her after all. This is my confession. I need to explain the whys and wherefores of that. It's a pity I have gone blank about the rifle. Where would I put such a thing? As far as I can tell none of my guns is missing. That's an odd thing. I shot her, but what with? And where the hell is it? And I didn't drive down there because the ute was in the shed on blocks, and I would never take Arielle's little Fiesta over that track. I don't even know why I keep the Fiesta, really. I guess I still believe she's coming home. I do, yes I do believe that. I know she's out there somewhere. The messages on the laptop were short and fanciful, scattered thoughts about unicorns and things like that. I don't know. Ginny's an artist – was an artist – she did pictures of fantasy creatures. I think she actually believed in them. Arielle did too. Unicorns were real to her. It sometimes seemed to me that Ginny sort of led her on a bit, you know. Owls and unicorns and hares. People have said Ginny was a kind of witch. I don't believe in that stuff, but she was – well, strange. Was Arielle depressed, what with the cot death and everything, the police wondered. I had to say I didn't really know. The policewoman gave me a funny look when I said it. Well, with Arielle, you couldn't really tell about a thing like that. I was teaching her how to shoot, to take her mind off things. She wasn't bad, actually. They took the laptop away, said there might be clues in the emails, or in websites she might have visited. Social media, they said. Arielle didn't do any social media. They brought it back after about three weeks. Said there was nothing there. They would have read my emails too, of course. Well, they wouldn't get much out of orders for seeds and fertiliser, and parts for the generator. I looked at Arielle's emails – there were four that mentioned something that happened when Arielle was out walking in the mornings. And answers from Ginny too. I suppose the police kept a file of all that. I certainly didn't keep any of it. They say things live forever in cyberspace, even on the laptop itself. Like ghosts and spirits. Floating around and coming back to haunt you. I don't know how to get them back, but maybe the police do. They did tell a story, those emails. I wish I had the exact words now. But anyhow, the story was this, more or less. One morning when Arielle was walking on the path through the scrub round the back of the Starlight, she saw up ahead a big animal in the middle of the path, at the bend. She thought it would run off, but it stood there, staring straight at her. It was a hare, an enormous big buck hare. She stood absolutely still. The hare stood still. Like a kind of standoff, I think. There was an eerie silence. She couldn't stand there forever, so she moved very slowly closer and closer, but the hare didn't move. She wasn't frightened for some reason. Arielle went past it, kept going slowly and quietly, and when she turned round, a few metres down the track, the hare was gone. She told me about this and I thought it was probably her imagination, but I didn't say so. You didn't say things like that to Arielle. I went along with it. You could say I was humouring her. Of course, she emailed Ginny who came right back with her usual rot. I think Ginny believed the hare was real, and she went on about how it's this symbol of fertility, and how it was giving Arielle a message – Arielle would soon have another baby. Arielle told me this – she was breathless with excitement. And I have to say she was extra loving in the bedroom afterwards. So I reckon I can thank Ginny for that at least. But then, about three weeks later, it happened again – Arielle met the hare at

　　　CARMEL BIRD

the bend in the path, and they stood and stared at each other – Arielle said they communed – for a very long time, a really really long time, like twenty minutes she said. Well you never heard of a hare sitting still for twenty minutes, did you? There was a strange white light. Then the hare nodded, and she knew she was meant to move on, and she did, and when she looked back it was gone. When she told me I really started to get worried and I thought maybe I should take her to the doctor or something. But what would I say. What kind of an idiot would I look, telling dithering bloody Barry Meehan my wife was seeing visions? He'd put her on pills, I reckon, and turn her into a real zombie. So I let it go. But Ginny Peach didn't let it go. Oh no. No way. Ginny was beside herself with excitement, and I vividly remember reading her emails (after Arielle had disappeared, I didn't read them before – I'm quite strict about things like that) where she said the thing to do to 'respond to the visitation' was to get me to go out round Moonlight Flat or somewhere far enough away and shoot a hare and 'apply the ears' to the soles of Arielle's feet. And before sleep we were to *bathe her face in the blood*. In the morning we were supposed to wash her face with strawberry juice and cowslip water. Then she would definitely conceive. Cowslip water? Arielle told me this and I rang Ginny and said she had to stop the bullshit for God's sake. It was driving Arielle round the bend. She could tell I meant it, and she said she would lay off. She was only trying to help. Yeah. Trying to help. Then she sent Arielle an email saying the creature would appear for a third time, and it would speak. Arielle must on no account reply, she was just supposed to listen, take instruction. It was dangerous to speak to a haunting sacred hare. You could quite easily be carried off beyond the shades. When Arielle disappeared Ginny actually came round here and started raving about the abduction, and I sent her packing. Told her never to come back here. Ever. And she never did. But she talked, and I heard some of the talk, and what she said was that one day Arielle would return, in some kind of spirit form, and she would commit an act of sacrifice. Well when I saw those paintings of the hares, and those creepy portraits of Arielle dissolving into the landscape, I somehow knew what I had to do. I should never have gone to the bloody opening in the first place. I don't really like art, but I was trying to be agreeable.

Anyhow I knew had to go home after the opening and get a rifle and finish off the witch. I mean bitch. And I did. That's the truth, the whole truth, and nothing but the truth. I can't explain about the gun. I can't explain about how I got from my house to hers and back again — but I think I must have walked. Maybe I ran. I just remember seeing all those bloody pictures of great big hares, and Arielle a thing in the background, and I saw red, and I killed Ginny Peach. She had it coming. The End.

*

Coda

But it was not the end. Three weeks after the shooting a surveyor doing work for a wind farm collective down on Moonlight Flat found, in a remote and ruined stone cottage, the skeleton of a woman. Pure chance. When it was established that these were the remains of Arielle, the mysteries of it all only deepened. She had died as the result of a blow to the head. No weapon. No clues? Was Dan Tasco a slow and deliberate serial killer of some weird and wonderful kind? If he killed Ginny because Ginny knew he had killed Arielle and left her out at Moonlight, why did he confess to shooting Ginny, and not to killing Arielle? If Ginny knew where Arielle was, why didn't she say? He could never really explain why he would kill Ginny anyway. (And for that matter, it was never clear why he would kill Arielle.)

I think I said there were interlocking mysteries here. Something came over him, he was not himself. He had to shoot Ginny. He must have been compelled to do it. Did he suddenly discover that Ginny had killed Arielle all those years ago? Why would she do that? And if she did, why not report her to the police? Elizabeth McGee could prove on points of circumstance that Dan did not kill Ginny. It's a pity to end up with so many questions. But all I can really tell you is that Dan didn't go to trial; after a time he simply went back to his sunflowers. *Fields and rivers of pure gold.* A photographer turned some pictures of it into postcards. There was a running hare in one of them. So far the building of the wind farm is in doubt. And out at Moonlight Flat people say there is quite an unusual infestation of hares.

***

          CARMEL BIRD

Art

Damon Young

Ben sat on a capital 'N', eating a large gluten-free biscuit. Ginger and date. Most of the biscuit was crumbled on the stones below, pecked at by seagulls and pigeons.

'Stop begging,' he said, swatting at a nearby bird with his exhibition catalogue. The pigeon came closer. 'Go away. Go work for Oxfam or something.' Ben rolled up the catalogue and jabbed at the bird. It came closer still. 'Bloody masochist.'

A couple of metres away, on the other side of the giant KUBIN, she slumped on the 'K'. Her hips, in frayed jeans, were wedged into the middle of the letter, her legs hanging over the edge of the ascender. Her fingertips were white. She was actually reading the catalogue, holding it high over her head.

He recognised her from the university. After the tutorials, Ben often sat smoking on the low brick wall outside the library. Waiting for their boyfriends to pick them up, his students liked to talk about Bourdieu and capitalism and capital and perspective and heterodoxy. And. And. Ben often saw 'K' walking by with an armful of folios, usually fin de siècle monographs.

Emo art nerd. With a Canova arse.

Ben opened his catalogue and looked at the pictures. In *The Swamp*, Kubin had sketched a brunette, naked, up to her thighs in water. Behind her: giant frog things. She was wading somewhere. Perhaps to death. Perhaps after death. Death was part of it, anyway.

Ben called the wader 'Lady', after a poem he read in his Honours year. *And at the closing of the day/ She loosed the chain, and down she lay;/ The broad stream bore her far away,/ The Lady of Shalott.*

For his final folio work, Ben had written the verse in glitter over a printed screen-grab from a German golden showers film from the eighties. His artistic statement quoted the philosopher Heraclitus: *One cannot step into the same river twice.* He received a high distinction, and was given a small printed certificate by the Head of School. The next day, he used it to light a spliff. Six months later he cited it in his tutoring resumé.

Ben lowered his catalogue to look at 'K', as if to warn her.

But she had left. Of course. Probably getting picked up by her boyfriend.

Ben wiped the sticky ginger onto his overalls, then ran his hands over his face. Stubble. The pigeon was now standing on the top of the 'K'.

'I know. She's gone.' The bird pecked at the yellow plastic. 'Just crumbs now, eh?' he mumbled. He stood up and walked back into the National Gallery.

*

Ben showed his pass-out stamp to the elderly security guard.

'Right you are,' said the guard with a slow nod. Old-school Australian. Red nose, thin lips, huge Rodin hands. Probably likes Streeton. Hates Koons.

Whoopee. Everyone hates Koons.

The Kubin show was in the old 'works on paper' room. Lines from the artist's first and only novel, *The Other Side*, were written on the light grey walls in a fraying burgundy Vienna Secession font:

> *I could see into the earth; in all these passages there lived a thousand-armed polyp; elastic as rubber, it thrust its tentacles under all the houses, crept into all the apartments, extended under every bed, disturbed every sleeper with its fine hairs and suckers... There were postcards too, in black plastic skulls.*

In front of Ben was his Lady of Shalott, together with a plaque that told patrons how to enjoy her. He remembered his professor's mantra: *From the mood to the technique, from the technique to mood.* Rolling his eyes, he stepped closer to *The Swamp*. Kubin had sprayed thick black ink in pools over the illustration: in and around the giant frog things, but also in Lady's hair, eyes and vulva. Typical Symbolist warning: the darkest part of the foreground was between her legs.

For a few seconds he saw Lady walking from the swamp, dripping from her holes. Around her belly were ripples. Around her eyes, black rings. More ink, running slowly from her face and thighs. She was safe. She sucked and bit him.

Ben was hard. Not fully hard, but what his schoolmates at Trinity called 'half-mongrel'. Uncanny. *Unheimlich.* Ben remembered the German word from his semester on Freud.

    DAMON YOUNG

Something to do with the Id. That narrowed it down.

Ben put his hands into his pockets. Nonchalant. He pushed his cock under the waistband of his briefs. Held fast. Lady stood there, eyeless, looking down at the water. Thanks for not looking.

'I like her too.' Ben turned his head so quickly his neck cracked. It was the girl from the 'K'.

'She's brave,' she said, standing to his right, looking right at Lady. She had thick black eyebrows and black stuff lining her eyes. A nose stud. And private school teeth and skin.

Ben smiled and whispered. 'Really? She seems mad to me. Walking in that water with the giant frog things. I'd ... you know—'

'What? What would you do?' She half-smiled, looking at him. 'Save her?'

She looked him up and down. Did she see him getting hard? In a public art museum? 'K' seemed relaxed. Either she didn't see the bulge, or she wasn't worried about the bulge. Either worked.

'No,' he said, shaking his head, trying to find a convincing lie. 'I'd wake up.' Perfect.

'K' snorted, smirking, and walked away.

Ben watched her arse. The denim was most faded between her thighs. There was a small tear under the right pocket. Pale white skin. Tucked into the jeans was a loose black t-shirt, which fell off her left shoulder. White skin again. Years earlier, he had received a distinction in 'A/S 214 Anatomy for Artists': it helped as he sketched her stomach and thighs in his mind. And then she left for the next room: *1937–1945: The Degenerate Years*.

Ben followed.

*

'K' was nowhere to be seen. The small room was empty. No chatter. No guards. Just more plaques and black plastic skulls.

Ben walked to the exit to find her – probably in the gallery shop. But his eye was taken by a small etching in the far corner. It was not in the catalogue. Odd. It was next to another quote from *The Other Side*: *I heard lumps falling. Soft, boneless masses came into being, female in appearance.*

He walked closer.

It was his Lady. She was standing on tip-toes on a rock, in

a shallow pool of grey water. Her vulva was large, and drawn in detail: fine black hairs, lips open, clitoris hard. Inside her was black. Her mouth was open too, and black inside. She was screaming but smiling, eyes wide and blackened. Lady's arms were spread out either side, as if reaching for something. Her stomach was swollen, and piercing her belly just below her navel was a nib. Ink dripped from its point, becoming the hairs of her vulva, the shadows on her thighs, and hard edges of the rock.

Hard again, Ben took his time gazing at Lady's body. Her breasts, ripped stomach, between her legs. Then he realised that the rock was a head; the head of a man. Eyes, nose and mouth were chipped into the rock. Kubin had drawn tears running from the head's stone eyes. A single line of ink ran from the head's eyelids to the pool. Taken in by Lady's naked horror, he only half-looked at the head. But something pushed him to look down. Something—

Oh, fuck.

They were his placid eyes looking back. His high forehead and thin brows. His long, sharp nose and upturned lips with the sharp cupid's bow.

Pale and faint, Ben sat on the nearby couch, his guts spasming. He squinted to read the etching's title: *Art.*

No. He ran out of the room into the gift shop and out to the boulevard.

*

The same old sun. The same giant KUBIN in yellow plastic. The same water-wall. The world had not changed.

But Ben was nauseous. He sat, breathing, on a concrete block in front of the fountain. My head. My fucking head. His brain was full of ink and skin and black blood. His mouth was full of saliva. He put his hands on his knees, bending backwards, and swallowed loudly. The concrete was warm against his back and neck.

Ben spent ten minutes half-listening to the busker play his strange banjo violin thing; to the water bubbling in the fountain; to the shouts of cyclists on the boulevard. Sparrows beaked at muffin wrappers and paper sugar containers from the café.

A bus carrying Chinese tourists arrived, and its engine

blocked out everything else. Did the job. Ben listened to the engine. Anything was better than ink and head and cunt and paper. Buses came and went. Tourists, too.

An hour or so. The concrete was warm. A breeze off the Yarra. More birds and bikes and pentatonic scales.

The horror was still inside. Dry tuna in a cheap sushi roll, sticking in his gullet. Ben kept swallowing it down.

And kept swallowing until the taste was gone. Then took a taxi home, spending dinner money on the fare.

*

Ben did not have the courage to visit the exhibition again. Not right away. He read Eliot in the morning, taught his classes in the evening, read comics at night.

But a week later, a little stoned, he walked from the university to the gallery.

At the information counter, a staff member with a Fitzroy fringe and Edinburgh freckles looked up. When she saw him – his reddened eyes and sweaty upper lip – her smile flattened.

'Do you … need some help?'

Ben leaned on the bench. Casual. Not threatening. Just a regular man asking questions.

'Yes, thank you.' Too formal. Try to relax. 'There's a quirky little etching in the second room of the Kubin exhibition.'

She said 'yep' three times as he spoke.

'I just want to know more about it. When it was painted. Who the models were. It's not in the catalogue. Probably something to do with copyright.'

'Really? That's … I mean, I can't imagine the Leopold … They provided all the digital images to our editors. And the curators … What's the title?'

'*Art*.' Pause. 'It's called *Art*.'

She pursed her lips and moved them to his left. Held them there as she typed. Professional thinking face.

'No, sorry.' Shook her head. 'I'm getting nothing. Jenny, have you seen a Kubin etching called *Art* or something? In the second room? No, me neither. Perhaps you're thinking of another show? Dali was in the same room late last month. Perhaps—'

'Yeah. Yeah, that's probably it. Ta.'

Ben had seen it. He knew it.

He walked back towards the second room. Not far. Volunteer guides pointed and waved. Patrons nodded. There was the grey doorway, with its burgundy quotes above and charcoal silhouette on each side. He just had to walk calmly to the door, cross the first room, and into the second.

He took a long, quick step and—

*

His hand smacked against a hip. 'Oh, sorry.' The torn jeans. He looked up. It was 'K'.

'You again,' she said, rubbing her leg. 'In a hurry to save your paper girlfriend?'

He thinned his lips and looked past her, to the doorway.

'Sorry. Just taking the piss.' She stared right at him. It was hard to look away. Odd blue eyes. Claude blue. 'Are ... you okay? You look a bit pale.'

'Yeah,' Ben said. 'I just—'

The etching was just around that corner. A few steps. She was in the way.

'Seriously, do you need to sit down?'

'I'm coeliac,' he said. More truth. 'And an idiot. I ate a big biscuit. Probably full of gluten. Hurts like hell.' A nice little lie. Neat. Simple. Easy to remember.

'Ah,' she said, nodding. 'My sister's coeliac. She found out on her third anniversary. Stuffed her face with Coles tiramisu. The stone for the anniversary was *porcelain*.'

Ben laughed by slowly showing his teeth.

'I'm Dee. I'm a fine arts student up there,' she said, pointing up Swanston. 'Inks mostly. I've seen you, talking with your students. Renaissance and Autonomy, right?'

'Yeah,' he said. 'I'm Ben. I'm a painter. Well, I was. Now I—'

'Yeah, I saw your overalls.'

Silence.

She had great skin. Eastern suburbs skin. Her pores were clean and gentle, concave. Paved and polished, not grown with skin and sebum and sweat.

'Can you drink coffee?' she asked, making the motion of picking up an espresso glass.

Well, well. Perhaps it was not masochism after all.

'Yeah, sure,' he said, looking toward the gallery café. Middle-

     DAMON YOUNG

aged retirees, and their bored husbands in short-sleeved plaid shirts. 'What'll you have?'

'Whatever I make,' Dee smirked, pointing up Swanston again. 'My studio's just down the road. I have a kick-arse DeLonghi.'

'Student life's changed a bit since my day,' said Ben. More teeth.

'It was either that or a used car,' Dee said over her shoulder, walking to the tram.

*

Once on the tram, they said nothing. Their quick, thick intimacy was cracked by other strangers. Dee looked out the window. He looked at her.

After a few minutes' silence, she spoke. 'I remember your first group show.'

Ben said nothing. He must have misheard.

'You're Ben Aaronson, right?' She looked back at him, over her shoulder.

He nodded. Still said nothing.

'Have I said the wrong thing again?'

'No.' He looked around the tram. Nobody he knew. 'I've just never had anyone remember my stuff. It's a bit uncanny. My show was based on my honours folio. Now I see the Kubin, with Lady, meet you, you remember the group show, that had Lady in it, and—'

'Lady?'

He shook his head. Idiot. 'Sorry, the woman in *The Swamp*. I call her Lady, after—'

'After the poem. No, don't freak out. I loved your mixed media stuff. Really. I borrowed Tennyson from the library the next day. *For ere she reach'd upon the tide/ The first house by the water-side,/ Singing in her song she died.* You really killed it. Here's me,' she said quickly, pointing at a thin second-storey building near RMIT. 'The first house by the stop.'

Dee jumped off the tram. Ben rushed, the doors closing at his feet.

*

He watched her arse move up the stairs. The perfect skin and teeth. The generous, tolerant parents. The torn jeans. He was

ART   135

expecting a share-house aesthetic, with St Vinnies furniture and Ishka hangings.

But Dee's studio was almost empty. Just polished boards, high, wide windows, three easels, and a bench stacked with bottles of ink, brushes and paper.

'Schmick,' he said, walking in slow circles, taking in the empty space. 'Very schmick.'

She stood on tip-toes to reach the light switches, hanging from rough beams.

'Thanks. How do you like it?'

'Sorry?'

'Your coffee. How do you like it?'

'Oh. Just an espresso, thanks.'

'Me too.'

Ben and Dee sat against the windows, on the floorboards. The sunlight behind them, they faced an easel. On it was a single sheet of paper. White string on the top and bottom, looped around the thick wood.

'You paint with inks on an easel? Doesn't it drip?'

'Darling, the drips are what makes art art,' she intoned, then smiled. 'Of course not. I paint on the bench with dip pens or brushes. Once they're dry, I view them here.'

'Why the paper?'

'You know, the eyes get bored. I cover the work with paper for a few days, then do the big reveal. See what works and what doesn't.'

He nodded. Smart.

'Do you want to see?'

'I'd like to.'

She jumped up, took a knife from the bench, and cut the top string. Then bent over to cut the bottom. In the sun, the white patch of skin on her jeans shone.

His hands would tug at her jeans, then lift her t-shirt. No, she would lift it. Anyway, no bra. Her underwear would be Klein blue and they would laugh. Then she would be naked and pale and—

Half-mongrel. Sitting down helped.

Dee rolled up the paper tightly, fastened it with a rubber band, and put it on the floorboards. He watched her movements. Fast. Meticulous. Elegant.

 DAMON YOUNG

Then Ben actually looked at the easel.

Then looked again. His stomach tightened. His hands tingled. Saliva filled his mouth. 'No,' he said, standing quickly. 'That's—'

It was the Kubin from the second room. Lady's arms and vulva wide. Stomach bloodied with ink, dripping down to Ben's weeping head. His face.

'No.'

Ben stepped backwards towards the doorway. His hands, shaking, tipped a glass of inky water onto the floor. It pooled at his feet, and followed each footstep. He turned.

Dee still had the knife in her hand. And when Ben looked at her, she was smiling. 'You recognise it, don't you Ben? You saw it? In the second room?'

Ben looked at the knife and put out his hand. 'What are you...? Don't ... Dee ... stop ... STOP.'

'Wake up, Ben Aaronson.'

The knife came towards his neck. Dee was fast, meticulous, elegant. A real artist. Ben cried, not knowing why. The ink's grey circle widened in the bright room.

***

Her Dress Was a Pale Glimmer

Marion Halligan

My father came home early from work that Friday and said let's go out for dinner. A surprise. We hadn't done anything like that for a long time, not since we'd lost our mother. He said it in his usual melancholy-ironic, soft-voiced way, but he said it. It was an evening in summer, the fierce heat and bushfires over, the weather warm, the evenings balmy; we would sit outside.

Ysabeau put on her best Goth outfit: filmy layers of black, long skirt, floating cape. She made this herself, Granny taught her to use the sewing machine and she's good at it. Her face was pale and she wore deep red lipstick. On her feet were mid-calf boots, laced up, not very summery but then neither was the whole outfit. I wore my favourite vintage dress, in polished cotton, with a pattern of convolvulus flowers in purple and blue colours thickly clustered over it. It has a neat fitting bodice with a scoop neckline and a small waist, with a full skirt both gored and gathered. It actually belonged to Granny when she was a girl in the fifties, she made her own clothes and this was a favourite style. She showed me the little five-sided gussets under the arms, which give a close but comfortable fit. It's exactly your size, she said, it suits you perfectly. This is because Granny and I have similar figures, small neat top halves with quite wide hips and curvaceous legs, but luckily with thin ankles, whereas Ysabeau is more straight and slender. Granny looked at me and sighed and smiled at the same time.

I remember the petticoat I had, she said. Tiers of tulle, straight at the top but the final tier forty yards around the bottom. In your terms forty metres, she said, near enough. It was wonderful, solid frills of tulle against your legs, holding the skirt right out.

What happened to it? I asked.

Your mother wore it for dress-ups when she was a little girl. It made a wonderful bride dress. But all those flounces, they got trodden on, and ripped, finally it was ripped to pieces. Thrown away.

This seemed a pity. I'd have liked that petticoat.

Some girls, said Granny, dipped their net petticoats in sugar and water, to make them stiff. Some had crinolines of rope, to make them stick out.

I thought I would look in op-shops for such a petticoat, but I've never seen one.

Never mind, said Granny, it's lovely and full anyway, it looks good like that.

I get all my clothes from op-shops, except for these of Granny's. She keeps them folded away in tissue paper. They were beautifully made, now they are beautifully kept. I think she likes them to have this second life.

So I wore my convolvulus dress, with a narrow band of velvet ribbon round the waist, and little flat ballerina shoes in purple suede. We are sisters, not much more than a year apart, but we look very different. Ysabeau and Annabel. Ysabeau has long dark hair, mine is quite fair and I wear it shoulder length, flipped up at the bottom, I'm sure you've seen fifties movies of girls with hair like that. It's not as hard to do as it used to be, says Granny, now we've got hair dryers and can blow dry.

My father blinked a bit when he saw us, then he smiled. What beauty, he said, and one on each arm. Well, of course, you don't want to take my arm, but we can speak metaphorically.

My father is a philosopher. Not in an isolated way, he teaches at the university. He's written a number of books. He is often absent, I don't mean physically so much, but in his mind. He is thinking of something, and doesn't notice the world around him. Whereas my mother was always cheerfully and perhaps frivolously in the present, always noticing everything around her. But my father was happy in his quiet way when she was there, and now she isn't he is morose.

I said we lost our mother. That sounds like carelessness, doesn't it, or maybe a failure to pay attention. You'll perhaps be thinking she died. And it is possible she has, though I want not to think so. Yet I can't believe she would go away and leave us without a word. We just don't know. She is lost to us, but quite possibly she is not lost to herself. Some people think she ran away with another man but that seems very unlikely to me. Perhaps she met with an accident, fell in the river and drowned, maybe, and her body was never recovered. I know of one person who thinks my father might have killed her, but I don't believe that. He liked her presence, her presentness. She was necessary to his universe, without her he is bereft. Besides, if she was dead, murdered or by some misadventure, I think we would know. The world would feel different. But maybe not.

We went to our favourite restaurant, at the back of a suburban shopping centre, near a park. It's an ordinary plain room but you can sit outside under enormous old trees and since it was a calm night, not windy or cold (for a change) that's what we did. Father ordered a bottle of local Riesling, he gives us occasional glasses of wine, after all many of our contemporaries are already binge drinking. He wants us to learn to taste good wine. The sun was low in the sky, nearly setting, shining under the branches into his eyes but he said it didn't matter, it would be gone in a minute. It took longer than that, but finally it went behind the mountain with very little colour, the light became pearly grey and the candles winked in their little glasses.

Ysabeau remarked on the light, how it was like sliding over an edge into another world. Father said, you want to beware of edges. Dangerous things. But he smiled when he said it so it didn't seem a very severe warning. The waiter brought the menu. Ysabeau who always says she's vegetarian ordered polenta with wild mushrooms and Father asked for figs with prosciutto. He told us how Augustine flung himself under a fig tree and wept when he was being converted to Christianity. Father has planted three fig trees, one after the other, but they do not thrive. It is a sorrow.

Ysabeau had put her phone on the table and it made that shooshing noise that means a message coming in. She picked it up. Father groaned. Not phones, he said.

I'll just check. It might be important.

She opened her phone, and read, frowning her brows together.

Is it? Father asked.

She read: like the notes that come down from a bird on the wing, to descend is better than to ascend.

Father repeated this. Lark descending, he muttered.

Is that one of those trivia things that get sent? I asked.

Do you think it's trivial? said Father. Maybe you should seek its profundity.

Mm, said Ysabeau.

As I said, he is a philosopher. Often we don't understand what he's saying.

                        MARION HALLIGAN

My phone was in my pocket. I felt the message arrive.

Mine said: The time of roses and the time of lilacs will come no more.

Ah, said Father, that's about loss. Love is lost and so is the season of flowers. Where are the snows of yesteryear, sort of thing.

We're too young, I said, for all that melancholy.

Who's sending this stuff? Ysabeau asked, but you couldn't tell, there was no information.

Clearly messages from the gods, said Father. They would use current technology. Now put them away, before more doom comes.

The wine was brought, and he made us pay attention to it. The edges of the sky were massing with indigo clouds, but the weather was warm and still. Occasionally there were little quakes of sheet lightning behind these clouds, flashing against the purple. The waiter brought another tea light. You can move inside if you're not comfortable out here, he said.

So far it is pleasantly spectacular, said Father.

Father's figs came, little furls of ham with the halved figs nestling in them. Father nibbled voluptuously at them. The insides of figs were supposed to resemble the private parts of women, he said. One thing about our father, he doesn't censor his conversation with us.

Ysabeau wrinkled her nose. You reckon, she said.

Not me, he said, it's received wisdom.

It can only be a metaphor, said Ysabeau. I've given up metaphors. They're a form of trickery.

Very wise, he said. They too often obfuscate.

I quite like metaphors myself. Good ones.

We were sitting at a smallish square table, three of us on three sides. The waiter brought another chair and put it on the fourth side. I looked at it, and at him, but he didn't say anything, he collected the plates. That was very fine, said father.

The polenta was nicely creamy, said Ysabeau.

We had ordered fizzy water and I drank some of that. The tea lights were little beacons of brightness in the dimness. It was not quite dark, the sky still held some of that greenish colour that remains after the sun has gone. A slight figure in a white dress came and sat in the chair the waiter had placed.

It was our mother. Her dress glimmered faintly.

Hello, May, said Father, as though it were a perfectly natural thing for her to be there, even as if he had himself invited her. She smiled, and gave a little wave of her hand at the three of us. I think Ysabeau was as speechless as I was. This was the mother whom we had lost, who had run away, or was dead, perhaps, whom we had been expecting never to see again. Joining us at a table in a restaurant as though this was the most normal of occasions. In the dim light of the evening she looked just as she had always done, pretty, not especially young, her skin smooth and slightly waxy, just as it always looked. Her mouth quirked in her usual smile.

Well, my dears, she said, what's news?

She always said that, when we came home from school, from university. Sometimes it used to irritate me, but mostly it made me think, like mad, what is news? What can I tell her? The three of us rapidly sorted all the stuff of the last year, what was important, what mattered. I said, Oh, life goes on, but Ysabeau told her gravely about her new boyfriend whose name was Alfred, she always said it with a tiny defiance, as though people might make fun of him, but of course mother didn't, she just nodded. The tiny lights of the tea candles sparkled in her eyes. Alfred, she said. It's a lovely Anglo-Saxon name. Alfred who burnt the cakes. If he did.

And you, Annabel, she said, yes, life goes on, but how, quite? So I told her about my year at university, so far, and how I'd had a poem accepted by a literary magazine, and she smiled. Father talked about the book he was writing, the trouble it was giving him. He'd always done that, and she always listened, she was somehow good at that, as though what was being said was enormously important, and I remembered walking home from school and planning what I would tell her about my day, constructing a narrative to give to her. I wanted to say, where have you been, what have you been doing, but somehow it didn't seem to be my place, I was the youngest, shouldn't Father ask her that, or even Ysabeau?

The talk rippled on, like a small stream, chattering in its course around rocks and reeds, a little brook, babbling, musical, inconsequential perhaps but of immense significance in its own small way.

    MARION HALLIGAN

She recognised my dress as having been one of Granny's, and was impressed with Ysabeau's Goth dressmaking.

Ah, she said, these things so often seem to skip a generation; I couldn't sew to save my life, no matter how often people tried to teach me.

Time passed, I suppose, but it seemed suspended. The wine glasses didn't empty, the main courses were not brought, nobody left or arrived, the sky remained that faintly transparent but lightless green. The sheet lightning continued to play about the clouds on the horizon. The small tea lights illumined us, but faintly. Mother's dress offered its paleness to the dark. There was a kind of peace, of calmness, that made you want things to stay like that and not change, and so they did for a while, possibly a long while, but then a wind began to blow, faintly, but making the candles quiver and bend and go out. Then you could realise how much light they had given.

Mother said, Perhaps it might rain.

Father said, Well, May—

She said: That wouldn't be nice. Goodbye, my dears. She stood up and slipped behind the trees. Her faint whiteness disappearing. Father half-stood, then sat. I realised she had never once touched us, she who loved to fold us in her arms, feel our bodies against hers.

I said, Is she coming back? What's happening? Nobody said anything. The waiter came and took the chair away. He brought our main courses. I'd ordered veal birds, not birds of courses but little thin pieces of meat wrapped round a stuffing. I looked at it on my plate, thinking I wouldn't be able to eat any of it. But I picked up my knife and fork and found it quite easy to empty my plate. The wind dropped, the clouds stayed at the horizon, the tea candles were lit again.

****

Significance

Susan Yardley

The first thing that confronted Faye Denaway as she stepped from the safety of the street into the unknown territory of the salon was a full-length, smudge-free mirror. She stopped abruptly, tiny swirls of hair clippings forming a dusty cloud around her canvas shoes.

There was no point in denying the awful truth captured there in floor-to-ceiling shiny glass.

She was middle aged.

It had crept up on her while she had been busy taking children to the dentist, pushing a trolley around the supermarket, ironing her husband's business shirts.

Middle aged. Halfway there. Autumnal.

'Hi, do you have an appointment?'

The voice shook Faye from her dismal reverie. She turned to the speaker, a girl not much older than her daughter, with a shock of pink hair.

'Yes, I think so. My friend Sally made the appointment. She said I needed a change. My name's Faye.' Her voice sounded shrill and brittle like an anxious bird.

The pink girl ushered her through a Gothic archway into the salon proper and pointed to a chair.

'Tristan will be with you in a minute.'

There were mirrors everywhere enabling Faye to take in the whole scene without appearing to stare. The place was a menagerie. Girls with brightly coloured crests strutted the floor collecting combs and clips and coffee cups. Boys with spiky quills and low-slung trousers threw their heads back and howled with laughter at something on the radio.

Water swirled, hairdryers whirred and Faye stared at her dowdy reflection. From her cream shirt down to her bone skirt and flesh-toned stockings she almost disappeared from view. Like a scrap of faded wallpaper that's been painted over.

Her children seemed not to notice her anymore. They raced in and out of the house fuelling their teenage energy with frequent raids on the fridge. At dinnertime they hid behind their lank hair and grimaced at the food on their plates. They asked her for money or for a lift somewhere, never for love. They complained if she ironed a crease into their jeans or bought the wrong breakfast cereal. She was an embarrassment to them or at best, an anonymous figure hovering in the kitchen with her hands cocooned in pink rubber gloves.

Her husband was pleasant enough, generous when it came to money, reliable certainly, but he had perfected a way of looking straight through her when she spoke to him. He murmured soft noises of acknowledgement and nodded his head periodically, but she knew he wasn't listening. Not really. Then would come a kiss on the cheek and off he'd rush to the office or to the squash court. Indeed, he spent so much time away from home that she wondered if he might be having an affair.

'Now, darl, what on earth are we going to do with you?'

It was Tristan, running his long artistic fingers through her mousy locks. She counted seven rings in his ear and two in his eyebrow.

'Maybe just a trim?' she offered meekly.

'I don't do *just a trim*. I transform, I create. Have a flick through these and I'll be back in a minnie.'

He thrust an armful of glossy magazines at her and disappeared. Faye thumbed through the pages staring at the doe-eyed models and their crazy hairdos. Was this what Sally had in mind when she had suggested none too gently that she needed a change? God, even her girlfriends thought she was dull! They were all re-inventing themselves with new careers, new husbands, or, in the case of Sally, a lover half her age! Faye still worked part time in the same old bookshop where she had started twelve years ago. Her boss reckoned he could set his watch by her, regular as clockwork, our faithful Faye!

Yes she was reliable. And predictable. Always on time, on schedule and on budget. Well this was where it had got her! Forty-eight years old and stewing slowly in a vat of beige.

A few surprising tears trickled down her cheeks. She rummaged in her handbag for a hanky and gave her nose a good blow. Looking back in the mirror, Faye noticed something peculiar. Her reflection seemed dimmer somehow, a bit fuzzy round the edges, as if she was peering through gauze. She reached out to touch the glass and gasped. The fingers on her left hand had disappeared. She grabbed hold of them with her other hand.

The fingers were still there alright; she could feel them but just couldn't see them. Her eyes must be playing tricks. She made a mental note to arrange an appointment with the optometrist.

'Rightio, have we had a browse?' Tristan was back with a look of weary determination on his jewelled brow.

Faye slid her fingerless hand beneath a fold in her skirt and let out a sigh.

'I'm so sorry,' she mumbled. 'I made a mistake. I don't want a haircut today.'

She stumbled to her feet, letting the magazines slither off her lap in the process.

Tristan rolled his eyes. 'You women from the 'burbs amaze me. Think my time doesn't matter because I'm half your age and I don't wear a suit and tie? Where do you get off?' And with that he turned on his Cuban heel and flounced away.

Faye murmured another apology before fleeing the salon, and then wandered a couple of blocks back to her car. She suddenly felt very tired, not her usual self at all. It was safe inside the car and the leather upholstery radiated a lovely warmth right through to her bones. It wasn't long before she drifted off to sleep.

She dreamed of a vast ocean where sky and sea met in a rainbow stripe horizon and where small, rhythmic waves lapped on a yellow beach. She was lying in the shallows and with every ebb and flow her body became slowly submerged in the sand, so that in the end she became the sand, shifting and granular, eventually carried away with the tide. It was the most peaceful dream Faye had ever had.

Her mobile phone rang loudly from its position on the passenger seat, startling her from slumber. Why must her children persist in downloading such awful raucous ring tones? The voice on the phone sounded cross.

'Where are you, Mum? I've been waiting for over an hour.'

Still groggy from sleep, Faye pushed her fringe from her damp forehead and checked her wristwatch. It was 5:30. How on earth could she have slept for so long?

'I'm sorry, Max, I'll be there very soon I promise.'

'Well hurry up, I'm starving!'

As she drove to the cricket pavilion where Max trained twice a week, Faye gripped the steering wheel tightly. She was relieved

  SUSAN YARDLEY

to see the fingers had returned to her left hand, but she had to admit she still felt quite peculiar.

Max was sitting alone on the kerb beside the entrance to the oval. He scowled as she pulled up alongside him, flung his cricket gear into the back, and then slumped into the passenger seat.

'Did you forget I had practice?' He was already fiddling with the radio, scanning the stations for his favourite.

'No, I didn't forget … I fell asleep. I'm sorry, darling.'

'What's for dinner?'

Oh God, she'd completely forgotten about the dinner. Maybe she could pull something out of the freezer. Her head was beginning to throb. It was difficult to keep the car moving in a straight line.

'Mum, what's for dinner?' His tone was more insistent now and he drummed his fingers on the dashboard in time with the music.

The car behind tooted, its driver yelling some obscenity as he pulled out and passed her.

'Mum, you didn't indicate! God, what's wrong with you today?'

She turned into their driveway and came to a stop underneath the carport. Max jumped out and climbed the back steps two at a time. Faye held onto her car keys and tried to breathe evenly. From deep inside the house she could hear Max and his sister arguing already. The throbbing in her temples increased as she entered the family room.

'Mum, Max whacked me on the arm.'

'Zoe's talking crap again. Can I have something to eat?'

'I'm not talking crap. He's always hitting me. What's for dinner?'

'I need twenty-five bucks for school.'

'I have to dress up as a famous person from history tomorrow. What can I wear?'

Faye stared at the blue numbers blinking on the microwave. She pressed the defrost button and tried to focus her eyes on the tupperware container twirling slowly inside.

'Dad's home.'

She turned to see her husband bustling through the back door, mobile phone glued to his ear. He nodded vaguely in her direction and then disappeared into the home office muttering something about a conference call to the States. Dropping a large handful of pasta into a pot of boiling water, she called out to nobody in particular, 'Could someone check the spaghetti in a few minutes? I'm really not feeling very well at all.'

The bathroom tiles felt cool on her bare skin but the hammering inside her head continued unabated. She lay down in the bathtub and let warm water cascade over her body. Faye couldn't remember the last time she'd had a bath. Baths were a luxury reserved for women with paid help.

Not tonight, however.

Faye lay back in her too full bath and wiggled her toes. She surveyed her forty-eight year old body as it almost floated in the bath water. Stretch marks, cellulite deposits and the odd purple vein painted a road map across her skin. She sighed, pulled a wet flannel over her face and closed her eyes. The banging inside her head softened to a bearable level and soon she drifted off to her ocean dream once more.

It was dark when she awoke to the sound of the smoke alarm beeping and voices in the hallway.

'Well, where the hell is she? She must have said something. Christ, that saucepan's cactus! Could have burnt the house down.' That was her husband, Mike.

'Dad, I'm telling you, one minute she was in the kitchen, the next minute she was gone.' Max, always the expert.

'Has anyone checked the bathroom?' Zoe, being practical for once.

The door swung open and someone switched on the light.

'Told you, she's not here.'

'She's been here, look she's had a bath.'

'Your mother never has a bath. Come on, let's check the garden.'

And with that, the three of them turned and went.

Faye lay very still and gazed into the tepid bath water.

Her body was nowhere to be seen.

She clambered out of the bath and stood in front of the mirror. Nothing.

No reflection whatsoever.

She opened her mouth and attempted to speak but no sound would come.

She had completely disappeared.

          SUSAN YARDLEY

Later, as Faye wandered naked and invisible around her home, she felt an unfamiliar sense of liberation rise up inside. She felt warm and unusually at ease with her nakedness. She did experience one brief pang of guilt as she watched her family bumble its way through the rest of the evening, but the feeling soon dissolved when she realised there was little, if anything at all, she could do to help them.

Max and Zoe sat slumped on the couch while their father opened the windows to allow the acrid pall of burnt saucepan to dissipate.

'What are we gonna eat now? I'm starving.' Max, of course.

'Maybe Mum's been kidnapped.'

'Don't be ridiculous, Zoe! Who would want to kidnap your mother?'

'Can I order a pizza?'

'I think we should ring the police.'

'And tell them what, Zoe? That your mother burnt the dinner and now we can't find her? God, they'd laugh themselves stupid!'

'But it's not like her to go off like this. Especially without the car.'

'Look, she's probably gone for a walk or popped round to a friend's place. If she's not back in say, three hours, I'll ring the police. Okay? Yes, Max, please order the bloody pizza!'

*

Did she really want the police brought in? Faye sat in the garden and thought hard. No, that would be silly. She might reappear at any moment and the police wouldn't take kindly to time wasters. No, she simply needed to reassure her family that she was safe. They would just have to cope without her until she returned to them in the flesh.

*

'Three hours is up, Dad.' Zoe hovered in the kitchen picking pizza crumbs from the box.

'Yes, well, I suppose I'd better make the call.' Mike picked up the telephone and then put it down again just as quickly. He held up a handwritten note. 'This is from your mother. Why the hell didn't someone notice this before?'

'What does it say? Where is she?'

Dear Mike, Max and Zoe,
I'm sorry if you've been worried but I needed to get
away. There are things I have to sort out. I'm not sure
when I'll be back but I know you'll all cope admirably.
I love you all and I'm sorry to disappear like this.
Mum xxx
PS: Don't forget to put the bins out.

Mike slammed the note down. 'Well that's bloody marvellous, isn't it? What the hell has she got to sort out?'
'Who's going to drive us to school? What are we going to eat?'
'What about my costume for history tomorrow?'
Faye looked on in disbelief. So much for loving concern!
Well, bugger them. Let them cope without her.
She walked out the back door, stifled an innate urge to put the bins out and wandered out into the naked city, naked and unseen.

*

There are many opportunities available to a person who is invisible and over the next few days Faye took advantage of most of them.
She slipped into cinemas and caught up on all the movies she'd missed, let herself into the penthouse suite of the city's best hotel and treated herself to French champagne in the spa, took free rides in taxis, spent a night inside the National Gallery where she had the Old Masters completely to herself, went behind the counter at the bank and into the men's changing room at the football. She sat in restaurants and listened to clandestine conversations, wandered through the houses and gardens of the city's richest residents and peered through the windows of its poorest. She watched a baby being born and an old woman's body being prepared for burial, was witness to a marriage proposal, an armed robbery and many moments of kindness, bravery and cruelty.
She paid a visit to the bookshop where she had toiled away largely unnoticed for twelve years and looked on in horror as new stock piled up, disgruntled customers walked out empty-

　　　　　　　SUSAN YARDLEY

handed and the quarterly tax return was left sitting in the correspondence tray.

She followed Sally and her toy boy into a hotel room and was gratified to discover that despite vehement claims to the contrary, Sally had cellulite, too!

Faye trailed after her own husband too, and discovered Mike was no more having an affair than she was. He really did work the insufferably long hours and attend all the dull work functions that he complained about. Poor man! She could sense the weary trepidation in his bones as he approached the house each evening. What new drama or impossible request, culinary disaster or teenage mess awaited him as he stepped past the overflowing bins and into the kitchen?

'Dad, there's nothing to eat.'

'Dad, Zoe's being a pain.'

'Dad, can I have twenty bucks?'

'Dad, the internet is down again.'

'Dad, we miss Mum. We want her to come home.'

Faye wasn't surprised when he snapped. Yelled and screamed and made the kids clean up and sat them down and drew up a roster and put the bins out.

Later he poured a large whisky and sat in the garden alone. His shoulders heaved and as he stared up at the pale moon, Faye heard him whisper something.

'Jesus, Faye, where are you? Where the hell are you? God I miss you. I love you and I wish you'd come home.'

*

Faye watched her children as they slept; their adolescent fears and fantasies translated into murmurings and troubled sighs. She remembered when they had been born, when she had first held their fragile pink bodies close to her, so utterly dependent that it was at once frightening and gratifying.

She wandered around the house, her home, and listened to its familiar creaks and complaints. She stopped at her bedroom doorway and looked in. Mike was asleep at last, his arm stretched protectively over the space where she normally lay. His breathing pattern was familiar and spoke of all the years they had been together, of a shared history with its own secret shapes and significance.

An invisible string tugged at her fluttering heart. She felt her way under the bedclothes and snuggled in beside her husband. She reached out and gently touched his cheek, the shape of her hand now clearly visible in the moonlight.

***

 SUSAN YARDLEY

Memories of Jane Doe

A. S. Patrić

She appeared in the paper seven times under the name Jane Doe. First the details of her body being found by the Maribyrnong River. Then details regarding the investigation. Speculation as to who she was. Appeals to the public for information. More speculation and no answers. A few brief mentions before she disappeared altogether. The last one was an article about crimes against women, on the rise, more brutal, increasingly unsolved, etc. etc. At that point, she'd barely paused between her transition from an anecdote to a statistic.

Ron turns the pages of a newspaper. Forgets about the ink on his fingers and licks the black taste of news off them. The black smear of it on his tongue. He must have been doing it for a minute or two before he noticed. And he's a chef for God's sake. To say he's been distracted lately doesn't even come close to it.

Ron puts the paper on a stack of them. Looks at those piles, some now as tall as his shoulder, leaning against the walls in his walk-in fridge, and still doesn't know what to do with them. They keep piling up. Filled with the controversy of a politician being discovered with paedophilic pictures on his computer's history. The Australian cricket team and its aborted tour of Pakistan. The celebrity murder of Katarina Sterling in the Park Hyatt. And going on about it, every nuance, every day, in every newspaper, ceaselessly, repeating every detail, over and over again. And nothing more of his Jane Doe.

Ron walks to the bathroom and brushes his teeth. Washes his mouth out with Listerine to get the black ink smear off his tongue. He sticks it out in the mirror and sees nothing but the faint green of the mouthwash. His skin looks colourless. Pale because of all the hours in the kitchen and sleeping away the best parts of the day. Pale, and pink. The look of uncooked chicken. He brushes and rinses again.

He came home from work one morning, it was as late as seven or eight in the morning, and found her in the bathroom, her head in this basin. Washing peroxide from her head. Her long brown hair in clumps all over the floor, and in his imagination, the walls, the ceiling, out in the hall and strewn across everything everywhere.

Because it felt like a disaster, even though she raised her head with a faltering smile that put a cleaver through his chest.

He pulled her away from the basin, and stared at her with her hacked short bob, like he'd caught her in the act of suicide.

Even yelling at her, 'What are you doing?'

She looked at him with that melted ice-cream smile and whispered, 'I wanted to see what blonde felt like.'

No way for him to explain to her what all that chocolate brown hair meant to him because he couldn't explain it to himself. She put her small hand to his chest to calm him down.

In a heavy accent, 'I was going to clean this all away, after. I never cause mess for you, do I?'

It was the day he knew something was wrong with him. Because he went to bed and he cried about it. Seeing her with short peroxided hair was part of it but it was all that beautiful long hair hacked to the tiles. It was a suicide that only killed the parts of her he loved.

Because it got worse. She started going out to raves and came home still dancing like she was insane with music that wouldn't stop thumping through her head, and going on and on about nothing, speeding or exhausting the ecstasy that was smudging her eyes with that dark sleepless shade of static. The different men coming home with her, fucking her in her bedroom, all vivid like welts and bruises in his mind, like they were pornos filmed using his daughter.

Yet he was nothing to the Jane Doe. Just a friendly man who decided to let her stay with him after working with her for only three weeks. So that they could cook together and enjoy meals with good wine. She could play her guitar, and he could listen to her songs. Encourage her and occasionally clap. Never did he take advantage, even though he woke up with thoughts about her and went to sleep thinking about her. And he was only ever appropriate, when he could have devoured her he was so hungry for everything she was.

It was after a great meal that she told him. Tasmanian Atlantic salmon caught only a few hours earlier, on the couscous she'd never heard of before she met him, with the fresh lemons she loved so much. Rich buttery chardonnay in tall clear glasses on his balcony and looking out to the West Gate Bridge, the water going out to a thin blue horizon, and holiday life down

     A. S. PATRIĆ

on Fitzroy Street buzzing up to them like the whole world was suddenly very happy. Everything filled in his heart, running reeling red and luscious thick – it was then that she told him she was leaving for Sydney.

Going to Sydney. With that smile. Her face already a golden colour from the early St Kilda summer. Golden like she was glowing with caramelised sun. Sydney. Going. Going. Gone but for a puff of smoke. He could feel the words in his chest like he'd swallowed the fish whole, and all the bones catching on his insides, and he couldn't swallow and couldn't move.

'You can't go,' he told her. 'Not like that. Just vanish.'

'How wonderful you make Melbourne for me.'

For her, like he was a fucking ambassador to the city. He told her he wouldn't let her go, and of course, she giggled sweetly. Even her laughter was confectionery. But he explained it carefully for his Jane Doe.

'I will not let you go.' He wanted to close his eyes but he couldn't blink for a few moments. 'I'll never see you again.'

It took a while before she wasn't laughing about it, and that quickly became a kind of fighting that threatened to be her leaving right now, right out the doors with her half-empty backpack and her guitar. He put his hands on her for the first time.

The struggle for her limbs became oily with things he'd never seen in himself before, rising with black mist in his brain, and spraying from his mouth until she was on the floor and she was bleeding. Not dead, but frightened when she looked at him, and afraid to scream. But then finding her voice. So he had to make a gag. Her limbs flailed and fingernails broke. He had to tie her down. He took the locks off the inside of his walk-in fridge. Rigged it so it could only be opened from the outside.

The idea was to put her in there and take off the gag and the ropes so she could start to think. So that this craziness could pass. He drank the chardonnay and started on the Belvedere vodka she bought him as a going away present. He wandered from room to room. Drank and sat on his balcony and gazed out to the blue horizon, which looked like the edge of a sharp kitchen blade just off the whet stone. He drank so he wouldn't think about Sydney, and the brutal marks across her face and arms, and all of this ending so ugly when it began as something clean and good.

He couldn't explain how he fell asleep for such a long time and how the dial on the fridge was turned to maximum. His intention had been to turn it to minimum and click it to off but that wasn't what happened. His hand had turned the other direction.

He finishes brushing and washing his mouth out. Nods at the reflection in the mirror. Nods at it again and again, saying, 'yes'. And, 'yes', again. And, 'OK'. 'Yes'.

He moves to the silver walk-in fridge he had specially built and fitted into his designer kitchen and turns the dial to full. Already so cold it hurts when he steps inside. He reaches around the outside of the door and swings it shut behind him. The handle and lock are still missing on the inside.

Naked and pale. Sucking in the crystallising air. He lies down on the newspapers. Wants to become a slab of meat. Breathes out shorter puffs of white. A clean taste in his mouth now. Death tastes like nothing at all.

*

Even at the last moment, before the car actually tumbles over, throwing the world around in a catastrophic spin of fragmenting glass and bits of plastic and crushing metal, even in that moment when the new Merc goes over its right side, Cicely thinks it won't happen. And as it happens, that this'll be something else. One of those things you talk about with a thrilled whisper in the back of your throat. Even as her ribs break under the steering wheel, and her right arm is all but cut from her body with the impact of a wooden telephone pole through the driver's side door, she doesn't see it. Doesn't believe it. Not now. Already. But she's still got a few moments. If she'd had a choice, before the pain obliterated anything, she would have ticked the box that read *immediate, painless exit*. But she's a broken, busted, bleeding body now and barely sees anything outside raging agony. It might have been beautiful if not for the pain and fear. Bunches of flowers on her back seat, the impact sending them tumbling around her, like in a snow globe. The flowers dancing floral rainbows about her eyes. A carnation falling to cover her right eye in pink. It could have been beautiful. And it should have been. Earlier still, and the reason for the flowers, there was Veuve Clicquot champagne and tears, even from Sure Ron, for the two and a half hats in

 A. S. PATRIĆ

The Age Good Food Guide. Waiters, for whom it was just a way to earn money and get good tips, couldn't understand what Cicely and Sure Ron felt during the night, when everything went fairytale, like the cosmos itself was whispering pearl music in their ears, *you are loved by the stars, you are loved by destiny,* calling them by their very names. But the fire from the ruptured fuel tank blows, not with a Hollywood explosion of dynamite, but a pop and whoosh, and the calm flow of gasoline spreads around her and the clean smelling leather seats of her first new car, with a gentle fire at first, which hurts far less than the shards of rib piercing her lungs, but builds to a crescendo. It makes her use her last breath for something not quite a scream, and barely a moan. And if at the ticking of the boxes beforehand, there was a choice for cause of death, she would have laughed at this one option that actually did her in. It was almost funny. Almost beautiful. But it wasn't a box. This is what happened – a duck, with a line of trailing ducklings behind, crossing the road just beyond the West Gate Bridge. She would have mowed the motherfucking things down if she'd been given that box to tick. Some kind of instinct made her swing the wheel to the right and then left to correct. Overdoing it; not used to the new car. The champagne didn't help. The euphoria of two and half chef hats in *The Age Good Food Guide.* That's what it was, probably. And that whispering pearl star music.

*

The black hours of no moon and an empty sky. The last trams outside rang in the hollow streets from the Esplanade and Fitzroy Street, with cracking electric claps for nobody. I wandered around Ron's apartment like a ghost that night. Thinking about how dead I felt. Feeling death all the way through me and having no idea it was so close.

Turning on the television and seeing a documentary about a man crossing Sydney Harbour Bridge on a wire. Thinking, *yes, Sydney, and yes, why not now.* I was free enough to fly over there like a bird. I'd earn some travelling money busking at Southern Cross Station and maybe I'd just sneak on a train going to Sydney. If they caught me I had enough for a fare but maybe they wouldn't catch me.

I watched the clock tick over until my head was filled with digital red numerals multiplying and subtracting. In the snatch of sleep I got that night I dreamed my head was the top part of an hourglass and my body the other half, and through my throat were the red hot coals of digital numbers from a clock radio.

I woke up choking and needing three glasses of water. I wandered around his apartment again. Endlessly moving around, like I was searching for something. He was gone so often I felt like I was dying in his stainless steel, spotlessly clean, air-tight apartment. At the restaurant again. When he came home, it would be after dawn sometimes, and then he'd sleep until four or five in the afternoon, and soon he'd go off again.

I watched the sky change; the light blue creasing the world at its edges. I couldn't get the idea of Sydney out of my mind. I wanted to see the harbour. I wanted to cross it in a ferry. I wanted to play music on the steps of the Opera House. I walked around his house, and then I went looking for a light-blue shirt. I didn't have any light-blue clothes in my backpack. It amazed me how strong and clear that desire for light blue felt that morning.

On Ron's wide open Fitzroy Street balcony, looking out across St Kilda Marina and all its forever furled masts, the West Gate Bridge, and the city of Melbourne, and its endless searching gaze across the half-dead sea, I sat a while and composed a song, overlooking the careening, flashing trams, sounding like dodgem cars at local fairs back in Serbia. Feeling homesick for it, and the wild trumpet music of those fairs as well, that drew up the wild bliss of life that was only over there in my motherland. That forced you out of your seat and compelled your hands up and reaching into the air for it, and screams of joy for life cutting through your heart, and the deafening whistling from the men all around, calling it to them, to their women, to their children, and for the world to know, God kisses the roots of the grass here with joy, amidst the hopping, stamping, skipping feet of the bliss abandoned dancers. Everywhere else it appeared in the world, it was something tamer, and as I sat there, that homesickness swelled my heart with a longing I knew was the lie of distance.

I was surprised to feel it cured moment to moment, by the vast opening blue skies of Australia and the brightest, crystal clear skies I could have ever dreamed of. *The Cure of Australian Light* is what I called that last song. Ron walked up from around

　　　　　　　　　　A. S. PATRIĆ

the Esplanade. He noticed me up on his balcony and waved. A smile on his face as he saw me wearing his light-blue shirt. For a moment it felt like we shared a life in that apartment but I hadn't put the shirt on because of Ron. It was because I wanted to feel the light blue of Sydney's harbour and Melbourne's skies as though I was already flying from one to the other.

*

Ron isn't generous. Even he wouldn't have said that about himself. But then there was nothing generous about the world either. And if that was true, then generosity was just another kind of weakness. There was a story he heard years ago about battery hens. Crazed as they were with their compressed lives, occasionally one of them would be cut and a spot of red would appear in its white feathers. The other hens would begin attacking that red spot, killing the injured bird. In the frenzied attack another chicken will have received a red spot and the frenzy would go on until all the birds were dead; or as good as. Generosity was that kind of red spot in the compression he felt all around him. Sometimes, though, someone good brings out the best in a person.

Ron feels that is true about the Serbian girl he drives to the city from the airport. He lets her change the radio station to whatever she wants. Changing songs he likes mid-way. Lighting a cigarette even though it makes him cough. He feels an expansive generosity around her he's never owned. Maybe it's the Eastern-European accent that makes him think of burning villages and barefoot winter poverty. She isn't pretty enough for him to be accused of ulterior motives. But she has beautiful hair, a lovely smile, and a laugh that resonates in his chest for minutes after he hears it. She seems to deserve a little generosity. His Jane Doe accepts it easily, and doesn't seem to detect any red spots on him.

*

Ice was in the corners of the windows. Lazy snow drifted down, and up again, in flurries. The black marks of skeletal trees made the Belgrade winter sky look like it was cracking open. But that was through double-glazed glass. And we'd cranked up the central heating to full and let it continue to blow the warm air around us past spring and into the height of a thermostat summer. I lay on the clean sheets he put down before I came over. I breathed the lavender smells of his mother's choice of detergent, fresh off the fabric. He was sleeping so deeply in that moment that I could rustle up a pen from my school bag, draw a heart across the left side of his chest, and write the lyrics of a song I came up with that week, in red ink inside it. It was just a shame I couldn't have tattooed that red ink into his chest. I knew this wasn't going to last forever, even in the most persuasive transports of our love. The trinkets we could afford for each other would fall into drawers and tumble further into boxes and then roll into inaccessible wardrobe cupboards, never to be looked at again. But I still wondered about permanence. About what stayed in us while everything else kept washing us out clean with lavender perfume. My face in his pillow on that winter's afternoon while his parents were away. Through the crisp white linen that still caught the delicious scent of this one person, this one man, this one boy, this one bit of love. Both of us naked and that being odd enough that it was thrilling. I would pull the sheet across myself and he'd tug it away and revel in just looking at me. His eyes full of me. His head full of me. His heart and soul too, but only for now. Soon he would wake and we'd have to give all of it up and surrender to the tree-cracked sky out there beyond the glass. When he woke, we kissed. Kissed long, like love lives in this shared breath of lips, like it might last forever, or as forever as lips can sustain. My love for this boy would fade, and his name would mean less, like the love that lasted this one winter, but it's the long, long kiss that is the heart he drew through my chest. The taste of forever which is sweeter for every moment it dwells breathing red lies.

*

Cicely drives in with another speeding ticket, to have breakfast in the empty restaurant. Her staff go about cleaning cutlery, polishing glasses, preparing their stations. She doesn't often change what she has for breakfast. Great coffee. Great bread. A homemade plum jam. Sometimes quince. Ron had introduced a marmalade he makes. And the paper spread out before her. She could do all this at home but Cicely loves being surrounded by tables, with chairs placed upside down on them, and to then feel them all removed quietly, and positioned below the

                         A. S. PATRIĆ

tables. To feel her staff around her in crisp white shirts and immaculate black pants or skirts cleaning down the tables with soapy cloths in the graceful arcing movements of their arms. To feel the building preparation. Everything becoming ready as she reads her paper quietly.

She's not to be talked to during her breakfast. Even for phone calls. Apparent emergencies. Until she finished her paper she'd receive only her manager, or her Chef, and even they would have to have good reason.

Today, Ron walks to her table. A pastry-chef he's had to fire summarily will need to be replaced. But he finds her sitting oddly still. Her cigarette in her ashtray, with two centimetres of un-knocked ash. Looking down into the paper, fixated. He stops by the edge of the table when he sees what it is she's looking down at so intently. Not reading. Staring at a picture. *Jane Doe* printed below it, as though that was her name. The newspaper asking for any information. Both of them looking at the picture until she lifts her head and stares at him. Her fierce eyes cutting through his face.

'Did you know about this?'

'Yes,' he says in a smaller voice than he'd like.

'Why didn't you tell me?' Her voice slicing through parts of his brain as he searches for an answer. 'She was living with you, wasn't she?'

Feeling lobotomised, he explains, 'But I told you she left. For Sydney. Had some guy over there promise her something. Because of a demo tape, or, I don't know … But she left.' And because she continues to cut at him with her eyes, and he has to continue to look at her, as though she wasn't doing anything more than criticise a point of the menu, he goes on, 'And she liked to busk around Degraves Street in the city or sometimes even those empty alleys, because the acoustics were good, she said. And maybe it was a bad lift she got. Because you know she liked to hitchhike. That's how I met her for God's sake.'

She holds him skewered, 'I didn't ask you that. Did I?'

'What the hell.' Not able to move, or blink. 'What did you ask me, Cicely?'

'I asked you, why, you, didn't, tell me.' And she knows. Without doubt. Watching him founder. And then she blinks. And blinks again. Each time clearing it from her head like grimy rain from her mind. Of course it was impossible. That comes into her mind. Also other thoughts. Like my chef and my restaurant. Newspapers and camera lenses. 'You must be shattered,' she suggests. He was finally able to look away. Let a breath sag his paunch under his apron.

'Well, she lived with me a month. I don't know if I can talk about it. She was a beautiful girl—'

'You don't need to talk about it. We're fully booked tonight. And busy is good. You just keep it together. This kind of thing is never easy.' He walks away, not having told her about the fired pastry-chef.

Cicely folds the newspaper. Notices her cigarette has burned out. Lights up another one. Throws the newspaper into the bin as she goes around the bar to talk to her barman about the cocktail menu.

*

There was something about people passing me that created a space in my mind I loved to fill with songs. I had to pile minute upon minute and accumulate hours of them to really feel it fully dilate. For the air to get thicker and be revealed as gas and the bodies and voices to blur and smudge through me with the oil of their passing life. I would play while I waited, and then, when it was open, all of these people passing Degraves Street could flow through me.

One day I saw a man drinking a latte and eating an almond biscotti. He had a crack through one lens of his glasses but he didn't seem to notice. He checked his watch every few minutes. His head filled with thoughts that couldn't find a way out. After he finished his coffee and biscuit he sat and went on thinking. They cleared his table and when he eventually remembered to check his watch again he got up and left quickly.

Maybe the crack through his glasses didn't bother him but I had an image of broken eyes. Glass eyes fractured throughout. I had this idea that maybe it was possible to look at the world through broken eyes and see everything fractured and exploding in a billion flying pieces, but pooling in our minds because all of us were the broken shards of an Ice Age Soul starting to melt. The music was the heat. I wrote words for the song but in the end let all the lyrics go and let it be something for the strings to

     A. S. PATRIĆ

sustain. To hopelessly reach for but never really communicate. Nothing I'd ever played was written down anyway. Certainly not recorded. I called it *The Broken Ice of a Melting Soul*.

*

Ron loves telling people about how he was headhunted. Tells it like Cicely Browne came all the way to London for him alone. If he's talking to men, kitchen hands or other chefs, then he'll add that for an arse as sweet as Miss Browne's he'd fly across any ocean, endure all manner of hardship, even come to the colonies. And he loved calling Australia that: the colonies. If there were women around, or he wanted to be serious, he'd tell them about the meal he cooked her, that brought her through the doors into the kitchen he was working in.

Which is what it was all about. Having a Dorothy break through to see the Wizard of Oz behind the saloon doors, pushing into the back of house, and not diminishing him to just another sweat-dripping guy with assorted stains, but a creator of something that could take a person sitting in a noisy room, full of feeding people, and transport them out of their skins directly into the mouth of pleasure, the body of bliss, and let them dwell there for minutes – a wizard with magic that consisted of nothing more than flame, knives and pots.

*

Cicely likes the Serbian girl. Knows that customers love her. The tips come in thick and heavy, more than doubling the wages Cicely pays her. She's pretty enough but there are prettier just passing the windows. No, it's that ice-cream smile and the laugh ringing through the restaurant like a bell sounding on the hour, reminding the patrons that what they've come here for isn't food, and it isn't wine, isn't conversation, or the views of the bay and its lonely trail of freighters leaving or returning, but a taste of joy – the brief savour of bliss. As simple as that, otherwise they wouldn't come at all. They could feed anywhere. But the girl tells Cicely she'll be finishing tonight. And Cicely's first reaction wants to be a slap to her face and to watch her nose bleed. She did that once to another girl that worked for her who wouldn't stop crying over some silly boyfriend, dropping tears silently on business suit shoulders like rain drops. Cicely doesn't want to give her the satisfaction. So she

returns to her reservation list without blinking. From the side of
her mouth tells the wog to hand in her uniform before leaving.
Cicely doesn't read the words on the page before her for a few
minutes, and wonders about her own satisfaction. Why should
the Serbian girl leaving feel like a blow? It isn't because of the
customers. Not because of the tips. But because Cicely really does
like the sound of that laughter. Cicely pinches her own skin at her
hip, hard, to get herself to focus. She doesn't let go of the pinch for
a few moments. Murmurs *everyone's replaceable,* and gets back
down to the work at hand.

*

I pulled my guitar out as soon as I picked it up from luggage and
played my version of *Little Boxes*. And then I played a song that
was only music and no singing. Had twenty dollars in Australian
coins in my hat in an hour, so people seemed generous here.
A man called Ron stood there a while enjoying my music and
offered to drive me to the city. Said everyone called him Sure
Ron. *I'll take you to the city,* he said. *I might even get you a
job.* I said, *yes,* despite a drop of red wine on his white shirt. He
didn't look too drunk to drive and his eyes became clearer as he
blinked and waited for me to finish another two songs. And I
nodded at him again and said *Yes, OK. Sure Ron, sure.*

*

Cicely drives home as the sun is just coming up. Exhausted
all the way through. But singing as she drives. She could have
opened her window to sing for the new sun beginning to rise.
The night had gone that well. She flatters herself that she could
apply the word *triumph* to it.
　Her restaurant is in St Kilda but she lives across the West
Gate. So it's a drive. Just after she crosses the bridge all her
elation flies away from her somehow and a bitterness rises in
her mouth that won't go away. It gets worse until she is forced
to stop her car. To get out and vomit. Between the heaves she
feels annoyed at her body, at her stomach, at the happy music
pouring from her old Corolla, at the car itself, which was third
hand when she bought it and now looked like it was multiplied
by thirty hands more. She stands up and wipes the back of her
wrist across her mouth, trembling right through her body.

　　　　　　　　A. S. PATRIĆ

At Cicely Browne's feet are the remains of the food and wine from the opening night of her restaurant, *Arcady Blue*. The culmination of over twenty long, long, fucken-long years of clawing-desperate ambition and white-knuckle dreams.

Shoosh-shoosh the cars pass. There's not much else around her. The most desolate place in the world is a stretch of roadside just off the West Gate Bridge. And she is stuck there as she leans over again and gets down to ribbons of acid.

Cars pass by, *shoosh-shoosh*. They keep passing like an endless metal river that is gathering a current. *Shoosh-shoosh-shoosh*. A relentless noise. The sound of a river in which drowning is not only guaranteed, it is instantaneous. You'd be gone before you knew it.

*

Her name is not discovered. Days go by, but nothing turns up. And it looks like nothing will. The coroner can't determine cause of death. Evidence of hypothermia, which was hard to make sense of, and nothing definitive. Occasionally it's impossible to get conclusive evidence for what has happened. We guess and we assume. There are questions, and there are searches. There is speculation and there is imagination. But her name is unknown. And days and days have gone by.

Naked. Broken nails. Painted a light blue. Some defensive wounds. Rope burns. Calloused fingertips, but only on her left hand, so a guitar player. Ring marks on her fingers but nothing indicating marriage. Not a mother. Hasn't been raped. And still no name though days have passed on a metal table.

*

The water moves past her, swinging her right leg out and back, her right arm, waving to-and-fro. But the rigour creeps in and it's only her hacked short hair, blonde through peroxide, that moves across the surface of the running river by the time the evening passes and new light finds her lying there, a nameless body. Face up and eyes open. Flesh the colour of concrete and the cold touch of fish scale. Caught on a river bank, out by the long, long Maribyrnong. A trickle of mud running from her mouth, open the space of a smile.

* * *

Sticks and Stones

Ryan O'Neill

*'False words are not only evil in themselves,
but they infect the soul with evil.'*

Plato

Paxza'ravrnam'bablla'tok

Early one morning in the summer of 2011, James Blackwood, Professor of Philology at the University of Newcastle, set aside the examination papers he was marking, and went out for a walk. It was a cloudless Sunday, and he strolled up the hill to the cathedral, waiting there for ten minutes until the hour. Although he was an atheist, he enjoyed the sound of church bells, and as he wandered away from the cathedral, he followed their pleasant echoes.

In a small side street, Blackwood stopped in front of a shop he had never noticed before. The walls were cracked and red paint was peeling from them like sunburnt skin. Even the graffiti on the side of the shop seemed ancient, resembling the symbols of a dead language. By the doorway, on a bench, an old man sat in the shade. Above him, printed on the filthy window, were the words *A BADDON*. Without the full stop, Blackwood was reminded of a sign on a cage in a zoo. The old man spat on the pavement from time to time, regarding the few cars and pedestrians that went by with barely concealed outrage, as if the world were his and his rights were being trampled on. Blackwood peered at a large cardboard sign taped to the door that read 'Seller of Clothes, Food, Sundries' and was about to pass on when he saw that the last word on the list, very small, was 'Books'.

As he stopped A Baddon rose to his feet and went inside, and after a moment, Blackwood followed him into the darkness of the shop. Though it was a bright day, it seemed that the sunlight was hesitant to come in, as if it were afraid that the old man might charge it admission. The cracked windows were curtained with dirt, and across one of them, running diagonally, was a disgusting finger-written blasphemy that Blackwood, godless as he was, felt obliged to wipe off with his handkerchief.

RYAN O'NEILL

On the wall to his left stood shelves of paperback books, mostly Westerns, and piles of old magazines that had the same discarded look as newspapers left on trains. Opposite these, hanging from nails, were racks of clothes, and teapots, pots and pans. Everything in the shop had a neat, handwritten price tag, and most of the prices had been revised up or down several times in red ink. The old man, Baddon, waited behind a dirty glass counter, watching him.

'Good afternoon,' Blackwood said.

'I was about to shut for lunch,' the old man replied. He had a harsh Scottish accent that conspired to make even the most innocent word sound like a curse.

'Just looking,' Blackwood smiled. 'Won't be a moment.'

The old man grunted and bent over to make some more price tags. Blackwood went to the bookshelves and cocked his head to read the titles. None of the books appealed to him, and he was about to leave when he caught sight of a broken-backed blue spine, which proclaimed in thick red letters: *Ten Terrifying Tales by JB Reid*. Blackwood pulled the book from the shelf. It was a first edition printed in New York in 1938, and the yellow, brittle pages were almost falling apart. The cover showed an amateurish drawing of a woman shrieking in terror at a ghostly figure. She had evidently annoyed the old man for he had gagged her with the price tag of three dollars. It had been a long time since Blackwood had read a ghost story. He was glad to pay the old man and leave the shop before he found a price tag on himself as well.

*

Dwix'bitud'slekdi'berbod'qadiv
Blackwood lived alone in a large L-shaped house on the corner of a busy street near the beach. He had been content there for many years, until a new neighbour had moved in, a rude, ignorant young man with tattoos on his neck and forearms. Often this neighbour played his loud music until early morning, and Blackwood barely slept. But that night, after dinner, there was silence, and so Blackwood settled in bed and began to read the book he had bought at Baddon's. The first story had the promising title, 'The Horror in the Darkness'. Above the word 'Horror', someone had written in red pen, *'cliché'*. Blackwood tutted and flicked ahead to

find that every page was similarly annotated. Blackwood disliked handwriting on books, considering it a kind of desecration. But after reading the first paragraph of the story, he found that he couldn't disagree with the judgement of the annotator, who had also circled it and scrawled, '*Sheer hokum!*' The story was so appallingly written that Blackwood only continued reading because of the amusing marginalia. Blackwood was proud of his knack at being able to guess the sex of his students, and even whether they were left- or right-handed, from a sample of their writing. But the writing in the book puzzled him. Sometimes it sloped forwards, sometimes steeply backwards. It was usually very neat, but at the most juvenile sections of the book it would become messy and almost illegible, as if the writer had become agitated. Only the dark red ink and the heavy pressure of the pen remained constant.

Blackwood enjoyed the comments of the anonymous critic enormously throughout the first five stories, until he came across a rather odd note beside a lurid description of a Black Mass. '*Not how this is done at all!*' the critic had written, and underlined. For an instant Blackwood had thought the writer was talking of the Mass itself, but then he realised that he (Blackwood had decided it was a he) must be criticising the scene as a whole, which was badly conceived and absolutely without suspense. A few lines further down the page were written the words, '*Stupid BITCH*' in reference to the insipid heroine of the story. The comments became progressively ill-tempered after that, and Blackwood found them less entertaining. The only positive criticism he found was a few words in the margin of a story describing the summoning of an ancient, evil spirit; '*There's something to this after all*'.

Blackwood couldn't agree, for this story was perhaps the worst of the lot. Still, he read to the end, as he had never left a book unfinished in his life. He had hoped the critic would have written a more extensive review of the book on the flyleaf, but there was nothing. Blackwood was about to lay the book aside when he noticed that the last page had, in fact, been ripped out. Considering the unseen writer's heavy hand, Blackwood found a pencil, and began to lightly shade the flyleaf, in case the writing from the missing page had imprinted itself there. After a moment he was rewarded with the ghost of a *p*, outlined in lead. Childishly pleased, he continued shading with the pencil,

          RYAN O'NEILL

and next revealed the letters *a*, *x*, *z* and *a*. It was gibberish. As he continued down the page, all he disclosed was five long lines of letters, making nonsense words. Blackwood squinted and stared at the letters, thinking that they might be anagrams, or a code. Tired, he was about to give up when he had the queerest feeling that someone was reading over his shoulder.

This was always a sensation he had particularly disliked, and it was for this reason he never read on a bus or a train. And yet, though Blackwood knew that his back was to the wall, he felt compelled to turn around and look. Upon the whiteness of the wall he saw the same rows of letters that he had been staring at for the last few minutes. At first, he thought this was simply an optical illusion. He was even satisfied with himself that he knew the scientific term: persistence of vision. But then all at once the letters began to move, like a mad optician's chart. The vowels and consonants re-arranged themselves on the blank page of the wall, so that they very quickly resembled nothing less than a face, with two *o*'s for eyes, a line of *i*'s for hair, an *a* for a nose, and a *w* for an angry mouth. Blackwood, thinking that he was overtired, went to blink away the letters, when the two *o*'s blinked at him.

Blackwood shut his eyes. He had often thought that characters in ghost stories behaved as if they had never read a ghost story, and he wasn't going to make that same mistake. If, when he opened his eyes, the thing on the wall was still there, he would calmly but hurriedly leave the house and find a place where there were lights and noise and people. Slowly, he counted to ten, and opened his eyes. The words were gone. Blackwood laughed, and got up to put the book away on the shelf near his bed. It was only then that he screamed. All his dozens of books were leering at him, their titles unreadable, the letters transformed from familiar vowels and consonants into an alphabet of hell. Hundreds of strange red symbols that were somehow alive gnashed and tore and devoured and copulated with each other. Some signs resembled twisted serpents and others unnatural orifices, whilst others still appeared to be crucified men and deformed children. At this first glance, Blackwood almost vomited. He felt as if he were looking at a bucket of maggots, or to be more precise, reading it, for the horrific symbols, though he couldn't understand them, still conveyed a sense of evil.

*

Dajuq'shroxnv'bljpo'todinaly'dewh
Blackwood instinctively looked down, away from the books, and found that he was standing upon a newspaper, and that the headlines were crawling up his leg. He cried out and stumbled backward, kicking at the paper with his bare feet. The walls of the bedroom gibbered at him, but between the transformed books he could see the blessed white of the bathroom. Blackwood ran inside and locked the door behind him. Kneeling down and breathing heavily, he allowed his eyes to rest on the white tiles. Then he stood, and, turning around, caught sight of the shampoo bottle on the edge of the bath. Its list of ingredients writhed and suppurated until Blackwood, whimpering, threw a towel over it. Blackwood was grateful he was a tidy man; his toothpaste and deodorant were shut up in the drawer. He didn't want to imagine what their simple logos had been transformed into.

When he had caught his breath, he began to wonder what he should do. He couldn't get to the front door of the house for there were too many books in the way, and he knew that he couldn't face what the words had become. The bathroom window was too small to climb out of, but it faced onto the main road, and he reasoned that he could cry out for help. When he raised his head to the open window, he staggered back, sobbing. He had forgotten the advertising billboards across the street which now displayed sneering, hellish letters that were five or six feet high. At the sight of them Blackwood could no longer control himself, and he was violently sick in the toilet. He lay facedown on the floor of the bathroom, exhausted, staring at the white tiles as if they might disinfect his sight. Finally, as an experiment, he began drawing the letter *A* on the mirror with soap, but he stopped at the end of the first leg, and smashed the mirror with his hand. The pain from the gash in his palm allowed him the clarity to gather his thoughts.

At first he tried to convince himself that he had had a stroke, and that this metamorphosis of words was some form of aphasia. But he knew, somehow, that while several of the letters he had seen resembled tumours and blood clots, they were not caused by them. Similarly he was certain that he was not insane, though of course he would think this even if he were. The transformation had begun when he had read the letters from the book, and turned around to see the thing made of words looking at him. The only explanation,

                    RYAN O'NEILL

then, was that the letters in the book were somehow cursed, and had possessed the alphabet. Blackwood spent the rest of the long night desperately considering what he could do. If the book had cursed him, he had no idea how to lift it, especially as he couldn't look at any other books to do research. All he knew about curses was that they could sometimes be passed on, and it was this thought he clung to as he spent a sleepless night lying in the empty bath. Fortunately the *H* and *C* on the taps had worn away long ago.

At dawn he shut his eyes tightly and opened the bathroom door. As he crossed his bedroom he tripped and fell against the bookshelves. He expected to hear the pages shriek at him, but the books simply thudded to the floor. It seemed the words would not harm him if he did not look at them. Blackwood knew that he had to find the book that had started it all, *Ten Terrifying Tales*. He was certain that it had fallen on the bed and he groped blindly for it. At last he found it under a pillow, and he forced himself to open one eye to make sure of it. A glance was enough – the woman on the cover was now screaming at the book's title, which writhed and leered at her. Blackwood almost screamed too. He ripped the flyleaf away and closed his eyes again. With bloodied shins he found his way into the living room, to his desk, and clumsily searched the drawers until he found a pair of old sunglasses. He put them on and slitted his eyes so that he could just make dimly out objects nearby and nothing else. Still he wouldn't risk looking directly at a book. Blackwood dressed quickly, and staring at the ground, went outside.

He hesitantly made his way to his neighbour's house, though at one point he was almost run over by a car when he stumbled onto the road avoiding a rabid cigarette packet. Blackwood rang the doorbell and waited, holding the torn page of the book to his chest. It was the first time he had felt glad that the man was in. There he was, with his habitual vacant expression, but mercifully wearing a long-sleeved shirt so that Blackwood didn't have to look at his tattoos of football teams and seemingly misspelled names that Blackwood assumed were his offspring.

'What?' the man asked abruptly.

Noticing Blackwood's sunglasses, he laughed. The logo on the man's shirt winked at Blackwood, who said in a quavering voice, 'I was wondering if you might help me. As you can see, I've lost my reading glasses, and have to wear these old things.

My friend wrote me a message telling me where I should meet him today, and I can't make it out. Would you mind?'

The man scowled and snatched the page from Blackwood. He held it close to his face and looked it over briefly before muttering, 'Can't read it.'

'Please,' Blackwood begged, 'could you look closer?'

The man stared at the paper a moment longer, his lips moving, and then he started. 'I've told you before, you silly cow, not to sneak up on me!' he roared. Glancing over his shoulder at the untidy hallway, Blackwood saw no one. The man spun around, dropped the page. Then he shouted something and sprang into the house, slamming the door behind him. Blackwood stooped and retrieved the flyleaf. Carefully, he returned to his own front door, stopping once to force himself to look up at one of the billboards across the road. The words were still capering and cursing and glaring at him, and Blackwood began to despair. Then he saw the *e*. It was very faint; the merest ghost of an *e* behind an obscenity that squirmed and tongued in front of it, but it was there. If the curse couldn't be passed on, Blackwood reasoned, then it appeared that it could at least be weakened. Squinting, he went into his house and fell into an exhausted sleep in the bathtub. An hour later he was woken by an ambulance siren, and eyes still shut he went to the window and eavesdropped on the commotion outside. They were saying his neighbour had gone mad, and had almost bled to death after cutting the tattoos from his arms.

*

Xi'ucumb'hiwpeqlo'upqojajdfah

The next day, Blackwood made two hundred copies of the flyleaf. It took him almost all day, for he had to shuffle to the library with his eyes half-closed, avoiding as best he could the nauseating litter, demented licence plates and menacing things that infested the shoes and t-shirts and hats of passers-by. When he arrived, it took all his courage to go inside, knowing what awaited him there. Thankfully, the photocopier was in an alcove near the entrance, hidden from the pulsating shelves of books. When he had gathered the papers together, he went out in the street and tried to hand them out. But few people would take anything from a bedraggled, trembling old man, wearing

　　　RYAN O'NEILL

sunglasses in the rain. Those that did accept a paper only glanced at the first line before throwing it away, although one or two must have read the whole thing, judging by the distant screams Blackwood could hear, and the fact that he could now clearly make out the *e* and the *s* in the disgusting inferno of the newsagent's sign. He walked the streets all day, but at dusk he still carried at least a hundred leaflets, and no more letters had become visible.

As Blackwood lay miserably in his bath that night, the only thing that prevented him cutting his wrists was that he could not bear to face the logo on his razor. He thought bitterly how all of this had come about through reading stories, and it was then that he had an idea. Perhaps people would only read the five lines of the incantation from start to finish if it was hidden in something else, like a short story. That was it! As soon as it was light, Blackwood would begin to write a story, or rather he would hire someone and dictate it, as he couldn't use a pen, or a computer. It may as well be a ghost story, he had read enough of them to write one, though it might appear somewhat old fashioned. Perhaps that was all to the good, for then the reader wouldn't suspect anything until near the end, when they had read the last of the cursed letters, and taken part of the curse upon themselves, and felt the eyes of the *o*'s over their shoulders.

Uowhe'hiehih'dahzoz'bega

Now, look behind you.

***

ALI ALIZADEH's books have been shortlisted for the Prime Minister's Literary Awards and the NSW Premier's Literary Awards. His latest book is the collection of interconnected stories, *Transactions* (UQP, 2013). He is a lecturer in Creative Writing and Literary Studies at Monash University.

DEBORAH BIANCOTTI is the author of two short story collections, *A Book of Endings* and *Bad Power*, as well an upcoming novella from PS Publishing called *Waking In Winter*. She enjoys weird stuff. deborahbiancotti.net

CARMEL BIRD has been publishing short fiction since the 1960s. She has published many collections, anthologies and novels, as well as children's books and books on how to write. Her *Writing the Story of Your Life* (HarperCollins, 2007) is a classic on how to write memoir, and her recently re-published *Dear Writer Revisited* (Spineless Wonders, 2013) is a great favourite with writers and teachers. carmelbird.com

KATHY CHARLES is the author of *John Belushi is Dead* (Simon & Schuster, 2009).

Born in the rain-soaked Pacific Northwest, USA, **ALEXANDER COTHREN** is presently drying himself out in sunny Adelaide. He studies creative writing at Flinders University, and *A Cure* is his first published work.

CHRIS FLYNN is author of the novel *A Tiger in Eden* (Text, 2012) and editor of *Terra Australis: Four Stories from Aboriginal Australian Writers* in McSweeney's *Quarterly Concern* Issue 41. His second novel, *The Glass Kingdom*, will be published in 2014.

MARION HALLIGAN's books include *Spider Cup, Lovers' Knots, Wishbone, The Golden Dress, The Fog Garden, The Point and The Apricot Colonel, Valley of Grace*, collections of short stories including *Shooting the Fox* (Allen & Unwin, 2011) a children's book and books of autobiography, travel and food. In 2006 she was awarded an A M.

KRISSY KNEEN is the author of the memoir *Affection* (2009), *Triptych* (2011) and the novel *steeplechase* (2013), all published by Text. She has had short fiction in publications including nerve.com, *Griffith Review* and *Best Women's Erotica 2013*.

P.M. NEWTON is a former detective from the New South Wales police force. Her first novel, *The Old School* (Penguin, 2011), won the Sisters in Crime Davitt Award and the Asher Literary Award. She writes short stories for *Seizure, Review of Australian Fiction*, and essays for *The Drum, The Guardian* and *Anne Summers Reports*. She lives in Sydney. pmnewton. blogspot.com.au

MARK O'FLYNN's most recent book is a collection of short stories, *White Light* (Spineless Wonders, 2013). He has also published in 2013, the novel, *The Forgotten World* (Fourth Estate) and a comic memoir, *False Start* (Finch).

RYAN O'NEILL was born in Scotland, and lived and worked in Lithuania, Rwanda and China before settling in NSW, Australia. His short stories have appeared in numerous anthologies and journals including *Meanjin, Westerly, New Australian Stories, Sleepers Almanac* and *Best Australian Stories*. His short story collection, *The Weight of a Human Heart*, was published by Black Inc.

PADDY O'REILLY is a Melbourne writer. She has published two novels and a collection of short stories.

A.S. PATRIĆ is the author of *Las Vegas for Vegans* (Transit Lounge, 2012), which was shortlisted for the Queensland Literary Awards. Other publications include *The Rattler & other stories* (Spineless Wonders, 2011) and *Bruno Kramzer* (Finlay Lloyd, 2013). He is the winner of the 2011 Ned Kelly Award and the 2011 Booranga Prize.

HELEN RICHARDSON is a writer and editor living in the Blue Mountains, NSW and a fan of genre short fiction. Her work has previously appeared in *Sleepers Almanac* and she reviews books at bookwoods.com.au.

GUY SALVIDGE is a West Australian teacher and author of the novels *Yellowcake Springs* and *Yellowcake Summer*. His short fiction has recently appeared in *Tincture Journal*, *Alien Sky* and *The Tobacco-Stained Sky*. Visit him at guysalvidge.com

CHRIS SOMERVILLE's first book, *We Are Not The Same Anymore* (UQP) was published at the start of 2013. He currently teaches fiction at Melbourne University.

RHYS TATE writes fiction and non-fiction for adults and young adults. He has recently published *Saving Davey Gravy* for younger readers. rhystate.com

SUSAN YARDLEY's stories have won many competitions including the University of Canberra Award, Rolf Boldrewood prize (twice) and the City of Glen Eira Award (twice.) Her work has appeared in *Aesthetica* (U.K.) and in various collections.

DAMON YOUNG is a philosopher, writer and commentator, and author of the books *Distraction and Philosophy in the Garden* (Random House, 2012). He is an Honorary Fellow in Philosophy at the University of Melbourne.

Also from
Spineless Wonders

SINGLE-AUTHOR

Stories that illuminate the ordinary - told with humour and generosity.

'O'Flynn's faultless ear for laconic Aussie parlance, his wry ability to turn a story in a moment from comedy to tragedy and back again, his exhilaratingly deft range...all this makes him one of a kind, in my opinion. A hugely enjoyable collection.'
CATE KENNEDY

In this short story collection, travellers on highways and trains are preoccupied with the lives of the dead, with lost children or with parents. A woman searches a suburban deadland for her missing mother. A rural family struggles on a land that fails to sustain them. A young man's attempt to leave the strictures of family life ends in violence.
A talent to watch.
WALTER MASON

In these seventeen stories, Melbourne writer, Mary Manning, looks at the ways people are shaped, or damaged, by their circumstances. The results may sometimes be humorous, sometimes tragic. Whether set on a tram, along a highway or on an Outback road?it is the journey, the characters and the telling of the tale that will capture your attention.

'Tart, tight and compulsively readable.'
PADDY O'REILLY

COLLECTIONS

What makes a man? In this collection of short stories, Pierz Newton John moves through the full range of masculine experience, with an openness not afraid to show men at their most lonely, sexual, loving, sometimes vulnerable, sometimes abusive.

'A startling collection…sly humour and memorable characters.'
CHRIS WOMERSLEY

This entertaining collection includes a romp of a novella as well as short stories and micro fictions all set in and around contemporary Melbourne. Sometimes serious, sometimes seriously playful –always written in breathtakingly beautiful prose.

"Be careful. These stories might cut you.'
RYAN O'NEILL

In *Permission to Lie*, Julie Chevalier casts a curious eye into many different worlds. Her characters ride the citybound bus route, spend the night in a nudist colony and wait tables. Quirky and beautifully-written, these stories provide insights that ring with integrity and compassion.

'A new voice in Australian fiction, wry, gritty, knowing and true.'
FIONA MCGREGOR

ANTHOLOGIES

In this anthology, our editor, Angela Meyer, pays tribute to the undeniable cultural influence that American TV programs such as Twilight Zone and Outer Limits have had on our lives 'down under'.

'These TV dramas,' Meyer says, ' were often metaphors for equality, justice, the nuclear threat and more. Though they were just as often pure, spooky fun.'

Due for release Dec 2013

If you like your genres with a bit of edge, you'll love this diverse collection of stories from Spineless Wonders. Features award-winning writers such as Ryan O'Neill, Jen Mills, Andy Kissane, Louise Swinn, Julie Chevalier, A.S. Patric and Kim Westwood as well as stories chosen by Sophie Cunningham in the inaugural Carmel Bird Short Fiction Award.

'Quality short fiction, packed with surprises. Prepare to be transported.' Marion Halligan

THE Carmel Bird
SHORT FICTION AWARD

PROSE POEM & MICROFICTION

What do our best wordsmiths have to say about Australian icons? This anthology takes a fresh look at everything from the HIH collapse to crocs, Margaret Olley, bush burials and the ABC. We visit a post-apocalyptic Opera House and spend Saturday night in downtown Byron Bay.
'A celebration of the many things Australia can mean to us.'
NEWTOWN REVIEW OF BOOKS

Here are short and clever pieces by thirty contemporary Australian writers on topics ranging from the eroticism of mash potato, parenting as magic realism and a tongue-in-cheek history of the Cyclops bicycle. Includes award-winning writers Michael Farrell, Keri Glastonbury, Judith Beveridge, Peter Boyle, Kent MacCarter, Erin Gough and Charles D'Anastasi.
'A treasure trove.' READINGS MONTHLY

THE joanne burns AWARD

Dear Writer Revisited

This book about writing and the imagination is essential reading for any writer, emerging or experienced. Re-released with new material and updated advice for the Twenty-first Century writer.

"Carmel Bird has updated her brilliant guide to those who are perplexed by writing. *Dear Writer Revisited* is a dazzling, humane and witty book which will be enlightening for anyone who picks it up, however experienced she or he may be. This is a classic account of how to write. I know of nothing that equals it."

PETER CRAVEN

'I first read *Dear Writer* as a nervy, secretive scribbler-in-journals 20 years ago. Reading this revised version I'm struck again by its practical generosity on technical matters - but am also inspired by the deeper, more complex conversations I think I missed in those early readings: about courage, about the urgency and mystery and self-discovery of the writing process. *Dear Writer Revisited* may masquerade – convincingly – as a book for beginners, but its lessons are mature and wise.'

—CHARLOTTE WOOD
THE WRITER'S ROOM INTERVIEWS

EARWORMS

Earworms are those songs with unforgettable hooks that get stuck in your head but Spineless Wonders brings you short Australian earworms—stories by award-winning writers that you definitely won't want to forget.

Stuck in a queue? Don't stress. You can listen to our selection of funny, political and thought-provoking prose poems and microfiction from our anthology, Small Wonder.

Got a pile of washing-up or ironing to do? Housework's not a chore when you can listen to short fiction from our anthology, Escape.

Commuting every day? Traffic jams are not a problem when you can listen to the latest in contemporary short fiction from Spineless Wonders.

Prices range from $0.99 to $2.99. Gift vouchers available. Listen to our audio trailers at

www.shortaustralianstories.com.au/audio

**Find out more about
Spineless Wonders**

www.shortaustralianstories.com.au